Mendosa's Gun-runners

When Quinn Mendosa's gun-runners steal fifty crates of rifles from Fort Stirling, Sheriff Rourke Bowman reckons that plenty of trouble will be heading his way.

But that trouble arrives sooner than he expects when his jailbird brother Dave Bowman rides into town and raises hell. Rourke has enough trouble on his hands, but when Dave offers to help him capture Mendosa by infiltrating his gun-runners it's an offer that's just too good to refuse.

Can the unreliable Dave complete his mission before the rifles fulfil their deadly purpose? Or will Rourke live to regret not running Dave out of town the moment he first clapped eyes on him?

Mendosa's Gun-runners

I. J. PARNHAM

A Black Horse Western

ROBERT HALE · LONDON

© I. J. Parnham 2005
First published in Great Britain 2005

ISBN 0 7090 7624 X

Robert Hale Limited
Clerkenwell House
Clerkenwell Green
London EC1R 0HT

Typeset by
Derek Doyle & Associates, Liverpool.
Printed and bound in Great Britain by
Antony Rowe Limited, Wiltshire

CHAPTER 1

It was only when a chair crashed through the Golden Star's window that Sheriff Rourke Bowman and Deputy Irwin Francis hitched up their gunbelts and strode across the road.

On the boardwalk they listened for a moment to the raised voices ripping across the saloon. Then both lawmen pulled their hats low and side by side pushed through the swing-doors and into the saloon.

Barton May was turned towards them. His hands were on his hips and he was glaring at a heavily bearded man, but from the wideness of this man's belligerent stance and the tone of his slurred oaths, he was clearly the worse for drink. Repeatedly, he was thrusting a finger in Barton's face and making him cringe with every lunge.

Rourke stared at the man's back. His eyes narrowed. But as neither Barton nor the other man was packing guns, he stood back.

'Deal with this, Irwin,' he said.

Irwin nodded and paced across the saloon. He swung to a halt before the arguing twosome.

'Barton,' he said, 'you're under arrest.'

'Ah, Deputy,' Barton whined. 'I ain't causing no trouble.'

Irwin snorted. 'Suppose there's a first time for everything. But this is the third time this week you've been fighting in here.'

'Yeah, but he threw the chair and . . .'

Irwin lifted a hand, silencing Barton, then turned to the new man. A hint of recognition tapped at Irwin's thoughts, but he shrugged it away.

'And what have you got to say for yourself?'

The man staggered round to face Irwin. The ripe odour of whiskey and vomit blasted at him. With one eye open and a shoulder held low, he looked Irwin up and down.

'Kind of reckon,' he muttered, slurring every word, 'that I want to say something.'

He rocked back, then rocked forward, his arms wheeling as he fought for balance. Then he swung back his fist and hurled it at Irwin, but the fist came so slowly that Irwin merely leaned back, letting the blow waft past his face.

The man staggered round in a circle. He thrust out a leg to stop himself falling, then threw his second blow at Barton. This blow missed too, but with a shrug towards Irwin, Barton slammed a sharp uppercut to the man's chin which snapped his head back.

The man stood upright, then fell backwards, his body as straight as a tree, and landed with a solid thud on the floor.

Within a moment, the man was rasping deep snores.

'I had to do that,' Barton murmured, raising his hands and backing from Irwin. 'He threw the first punch and he was trying to pick a fight before that.'

Irwin winced and turned to the bartender, who considered the fallen man, then Barton. He shrugged and provided a nod.

'Yeah,' he said. 'Barton wasn't interested in no fight. But that man was set on raising hell from the moment he came in here.'

As Irwin nodded, Rourke sauntered across the saloon to join him.

'You just got lucky, Barton,' he said. 'We ain't arresting you. But that was your last warning. Any more trouble and you're facing more than one night in a cell.'

Barton muttered to himself, then paced over the fallen man. As he shuffled to the bar, Rourke grabbed the fallen man's legs while Irwin levered his hands under his armpits.

'Has he got any money, Sheriff?' the bartender shouted, pointing at the jagged shards of glass in the window frame. 'Because I got me a broken window to pay for.'

'While this man's in my custody, you ain't getting his money.'

'Then how do I pay for a new window?'

Rourke released the supine man's leg to tip back his hat.

'I just reckon it'd be easier on all of us if you didn't

get your windows broken in the first place.' Rourke winked at Irwin. 'So the next time that someone as drunk as this piece of saloon trash wants a drink, don't serve him.'

The bartender snorted. 'But that'd get my windows broken even faster.'

Rourke laughed. 'Perhaps, but that just ain't my problem.'

He nodded to Irwin and, on the count of three, they lifted the supine man. They shuffled their hands to grab a firm grip, then walked him out of the saloon and down the boardwalk to the sheriff's office.

With some manoeuvring to avoid banging the man's head, they edged into the office.

At the back of the office were three cells, all of which were unoccupied. Irwin kicked open the central cell. Then they slipped inside and dropped the man on the bunk.

Through all these manoeuvrings the man never stirred from his slumbers, maintaining an incessant snoring instead.

With his hands on his hips, Irwin whistled under his breath while Rourke rolled his shoulders, relieving his strained muscles, and sauntered from the cell.

Irwin locked the cell door, then leaned on the bars.

'Any idea who this ugly varmint is?' he asked.

Rourke joined Irwin in considering the snoring man.

'Yup,' he said. 'His name is Dave.'

'How do you know that?'
Rourke pushed from the bars and snorted.
'Because he's my brother.'

CHAPTER 2

'How much longer are we waiting?' Irwin muttered as he peered down Snakepass Gully.

'Patience,' Rourke said. He lifted a hand to shield his eyes from the early morning sun, but let a smile emerge for the first time today. For the last hour Rourke had given Irwin an account of all the trouble Dave had caused and now their conversation had at last turned to the only important matter currently troubling them.

Two weeks ago, Quinn Mendosa and his gang of outlaws had stolen fifty crates of rifles from Fort Stirling. Since then, there had been sporadic and probably dubious sightings of the gun-runners, but none was fresh enough to let Rourke follow Mendosa's trail.

Although by now Mendosa had probably sold the rifles to the wrong people and left the state, Rourke hoped that both Mendosa and the rifles were still on his territory.

But every passing day eroded that hope.

Marshal Jake T. Devine had been tasked with

bringing Mendosa to justice, and was roaming back and forth across Rourke's territory. This alone had strengthened Rourke's and Irwin's conviction that if anyone should capture Mendosa and ensure those rifles wouldn't be used to take the lives of innocent homesteaders, it'd be them.

Staking out the trail to Lincoln was a desperate act, but as their patrols hadn't located Mendosa, it was their only option. So for the last four hours the lawmen had hidden half-way up the side of Snakepass Gully.

But so far this morning, nobody had headed down the gully.

'I got patience,' Irwin said, rubbing his dust-coated elbows. 'I just don't like lying on rock all day.'

'Riding round searching for trails and hoping we might get lucky ain't got us anywhere. We have to try something different.'

'You're right, but riding round is a whole lot easier than getting slow-roasted in the sun waiting for some rattler to bite.'

'Perhaps you're right,' Rourke said. 'Go scout around for a while.'

Irwin nodded and the two lawmen headed for their horses, but when they'd mounted them, Rourke tipped his hat to Irwin and turned towards Stone Creek.

'You not coming?' Irwin asked.

'Nope. Got me that family matter back in Stone Creek.' Rourke turned back and sighed. 'And I'd sooner face Mendosa than face that.'

*

11

'So,' Rourke said as he glared at Dave through the cell bars, 'why have you returned?'

Dave leaned back on his bunk. From under his lowered hat he stared at Rourke. The low sun glinting off the cell bars rippled across his grimed cheeks.

'To see whether you've taken good care of the family home.' He flashed Rourke a smile.

Rourke sneered. 'You don't care about *my* home.'

'I suppose I don't.' Dave leaned forward and held his arms wide. Another smile emerged. 'But do I need an excuse to see my one and only brother for the first time in ten years?'

'It's fifteen years.'

'My mistake.' Dave's smile grew into a grin. 'But the sentiment's the same.'

Rourke kicked the base of the cell bars, then shrugged.

'Whether it's ten years, fifteen years, or a lifetime, I still don't believe you wanted to see me.'

Dave glanced into the adjoining cell and when his gaze returned to centre on Rourke, his bearded jaw was set firm and no hint of his former smile remained.

'Then I'll give you the truth. I was heading to Denver and it was a fifty-mile detour to avoid Stone Creek. So it was easier to see you than not.'

'I don't believe that.' Rourke rattled the locked cell door. 'When I found you, it seemed to me that you were just drinking too much and fighting too much in the Golden Star.'

Dave clapped his mouth open and closed and kneaded his forehead.

'You don't need to remind me of that. But the truth is, I only went in the saloon for a drink to get the courage to see you. And then I reckoned that after all those years away, I needed a bit more courage, then a bit more, then . . .'

'Then you picked a fight.'

Dave rubbed his chin. 'Well, I got talking to that old varmint Barton May. He didn't recognize me, but after a few drinks and a few arguments I fancied knocking him down. Then he threw a chair at me and—'

'*You* threw the chair at him.'

Dave shrugged. 'Either way, you blaming me for fighting with Barton?'

Rourke glared at Dave, trying to keep any trace of good humour from his expression, but as Dave continued to look at him, he let a smile appear.

'I ain't blaming you for fighting with Barton. That man has an endless capacity to rile people.' Rourke rubbed his mouth with the back of his hand, wiping away the smile. 'But you always could find an excuse for your actions. And just like before, it wasn't your fault.'

Rourke sauntered to his desk and returned with the cell key. He unlocked the door and swung it open, then leaned back against the doorframe with his hand held to the side.

Dave raised his eyebrows. 'You letting me go? Because I ain't looking for no favouritism.'

'And you ain't getting any from me. I'm treating you like I treat all itinerant troublemakers. You can leave town in your own time.' Rourke tipped back his hat. 'But if you take too long about it, I'll run you out of town.'

'Don't you want to spend time with your only brother?'

'Nope. Spent enough time with you long before you left home.'

Dave sighed and slapped both hands down on his knees.

'In that case, I got no reason to stay.'

Dave levered himself to his feet and walked to the cell door. Rourke stood aside to let him pass. From the corner of his eye Dave glanced at Rourke as he slipped through the doorway, but Rourke had hardened his jaw and just returned a blank stare.

With a shoulder down, Dave sauntered half-way to the office door, then stopped.

Rourke sighed. 'Don't waste your time looking for something that ain't here. We got nothing to say to each other.'

'You got no reason to want to see me. And if truth be known, I got no reason to want to see you either.' Dave shuffled round to look at Rourke, his eyes cold. 'But I really do have a hankering to see my old home. Whatever you think of me, I reckon you got no right to deny me that.'

Rourke breathed deeply, then swung the cell door closed so that it crashed against the bars with a dull clang.

'Suppose I haven't.' Rourke strode past Dave and headed for the office door. 'I'll take you out to see it.'

'And I ain't looking for no charity or anything, but

I ain't ate much for the last two days and . . .'

Rourke swung to a halt and turned.

'And what?'

'And I'm kind of hungry.' Dave rubbed his flat stomach, then swung his hat from his head and smiled. 'And I ain't got much money after drinking most of it away last night.'

Rourke opened his mouth, determined to refuse this plea, but his gaze roved over Dave's wispy hair and in a nervous gesture, he brushed back his hat to feel the edges of his own receding hairline.

'Perhaps,' he murmured, 'as we're kin, you can stay for a meal.'

'Obliged.'

Rourke sighed, then shook his head and held his hands wide.

'And I still have the old barn, so if you need somewhere to sleep for the night . . .'

'I'd like that.' Dave raised a finger. 'Just for the one night, mind.'

Rourke nodded. 'Just for the one night.'

'Kind of reckoned you wouldn't take to farming.' Dave tipped back his hat and smiled. 'Seems I was right.'

Rourke drew his horse to a halt on the edge of what had once been the Bowman family land. Ahead, the thirty-acre field was now Walt Silt's land. The other two fields were now open to Josh Lester's cattle.

Only the barn and house remained of the once substantial area of pasture and farmed land that their

15

father had spent his life building.

'Nope,' Rourke said. He leaned forward in the saddle, but looked at Dave from the corner of his eye. 'The law was more to my liking. I prefer to get my hands dirty rounding up good-for-nothings.'

'How long you been a lawman?'

'I was Sheriff Ogden's deputy until he died in Dirtwood.' Rourke sighed. 'And you, what have you been doing?'

'Been around, earning my keep, then moving on.'

'That ain't much detail for fifteen years away.'

'It ain't, but I've never had much to say for myself.'

'What? You've never had . . .' Rourke snorted as he contemplated Dave's wide grin, then shook the reins and hurried on ahead to the house.

Celeste was outside pumping water from the well. She glanced up and nodded to them both, Dave tipping his hat, then returned to pumping.

With a shake of his head, Rourke dismounted and hurried to her side. He prised her hand from the pump and began his own vigorous pumping motion.

She stood back, a hand over her belly, although as yet there was no sign of a swelling.

'I'm not an invalid,' she muttered.

'Quit whining, woman,' he said, then looked up to face a slap on the arm, but he just smiled and continued pumping.

When the bucket was brimming, they both glanced at it, but Celeste grabbed the handle first and swung it away from Rourke's grasping hand. Her sudden lunge sloshed half of the water on the ground.

She stared at the spilt water, then turned back to Rourke.

'See what happens when you get in the way.'

Rourke shrugged, enjoying the argument they'd had every day for the last month and which, based on the experience of their firstborn, Harlan, and their two losses, he'd repeatedly lose for the next five months. But then he stood tall and pointed at Dave.

'Ain't no time for that argument,' he said. 'We have a visitor.'

Celeste lowered the bucket and faced Dave, who swung down from his horse and shuffled towards them. He swung his hat from his head and held it before him.

'Howdy, sister-in-law,' he said.

'Sister-in-law?' She narrowed her eyes, then nodded. 'So you're Dave.'

'In the flesh. Twice as large and—'

'In your case,' Rourke murmured, 'twice as ugly.'

Dave laughed, Rourke joining in for a single snort. Celeste looked at each man in turn.

'It's the old family joke,' Dave said. He looked over the house. 'And the old family house looks pretty much the same.'

Rourke considered Dave, then strode to his side and led him a few paces from Celeste.

'It is,' he said, lowering his voice. 'But you got no reason to be interested about what's inside. Your visit can go well, but only if you behave a whole lot better than you behaved in the Golden Star. So you stay out of the house. I ain't got much of a fence, so when you look around, don't stray across land that ain't mine

17

any more. If you want to rest up, you'll stay in the barn. When you eat, you'll eat in the barn.'

'So many rules.' Dave whistled through his teeth. 'Life here ain't changed in fifteen years.'

Dave smiled, his gaze searching Rourke's eyes, probably for a hint of amusement, but Rourke just pointed to the barn.

'Barn's over there,' he said.

Dave nodded to Rourke, then to Celeste. He swung his hat on his head and led his horse to the barn.

Celeste joined Rourke to watch him leave. When Dave sauntered into the barn, she turned to him.

'You don't look pleased to see him.'

'That's because he ain't much to be proud of,' Rourke murmured.

'You've always said that he's a worthless varmint, but he doesn't seem that bad.'

Rourke turned to her and folded his arms.

'He is. I get reports about troublemakers to watch out for. His name has occurred plenty of times.' Rourke shook his head. 'By my reckoning he's spent more of the last fifteen years in jail than out of it.'

Celeste sighed. 'When you became a lawman, you said you'd treat all men fairly, regardless of who they are. And I'm proud that you always have. So why are you treating your own brother differently?'

For long moments Rourke didn't reply. Then he tipped back his hat to run his hand through his sparse hair.

'I'll give you the most recent reason. I asked him what he'd been doing, and he avoided the question.'

'You don't expect him to mention the time he spent in jail, do you?'

'Perhaps not. But either way, I reckon it just means he ain't learnt to take responsibility for his actions.' Rourke turned to glare at the barn. 'And I ain't wasting my time teaching him how to do that.'

CHAPTER 3

While Rourke was away from Stone Creek searching for Mendosa's trail, he expected Dave to violate his instructions.

So he requested, as strongly as he dared, that Celeste didn't stray far from her rifle before she went into town to work in Foster Cartwright's store. Then he told Walt Silt and Josh Lester about his visitor, and gave them permission to stop Dave causing trouble in any way they saw fit.

Even with those precautions, he asked Deputy Francis to ride past his house during the day.

Although these precautions rested Rourke's mind, they paid no obvious dividend. When, at the end of another day of fruitless searching, Rourke checked with everyone, they all said that Dave had only sauntered around the edge of Rourke's land, all the time looking as if he was visiting a place with plenty of memories and was enjoying reliving those memories.

When Rourke returned home, Celeste also voiced this opinion, but Rourke merely grunted in a noncommittal manner and played with Harlan instead.

When the dinner was ready, Celeste laid three plates on the table and fingered a fourth. She looked at Rourke, but Rourke shook his head, so she placed it on the table and piled two ladles of stew on it.

'Harlan,' she said, 'take this meal out to the man in the barn.'

'And don't talk to him,' Rourke muttered.

Harlan climbed down from his chair and lifted the plate.

'Why?' he asked.

'Because he ain't staying,' Rourke murmured, 'and he ain't got nothing to say to you that you want to hear.'

'Who is he?'

'Dave . . . just Dave.'

Harlan edged a pace from the table, his tongue clamped between his lips as he avoided spilling the dinner with exaggerated care.

'And what's he doing in our barn?'

Rourke gritted his teeth and took a deep breath to avoid the snapped response he wanted to utter, but in the pause, Celeste coughed.

'The more questions you ask,' she said, patting Harlan's shoulder, 'the colder your dinner will be when you return.'

Harlan nodded, then hurried to the door.

When Harlan slipped outside, Celeste turned to Rourke and shook her head.

'You could have taken his meal to him.'

Rourke nodded. 'Yeah. I could have.'

*

In the doorway to the barn, Harlan looked around. His gaze picked out the man sitting by the back wall, whittling on a stick.

'Is that my dinner?' Dave asked.

'Yup.'

Harlan gulped, wondering if his response broke his pa's order not to speak to Dave. But he shrugged and walked across the barn. With both hands, he held the plate out to Dave.

Dave glanced at the steaming stew, then looked up at him. 'And are you my nephew?'

Harlan placed the plate on the ground before Dave. He rubbed his forehead, struggling with his dilemma, but then decided that as he'd already disobeyed his pa, talking again wouldn't cause more trouble. He smiled.

'Ain't sure what a nephew is.'

'It means I'm your pa's brother. We're kin.'

'Ain't had kin before – aside from my ma and pa. And aside from my sister, or maybe brother, who's coming soon.'

'That's a whole mess of kin. You got room for an uncle?'

Harlan considered a moment, then nodded.

'I reckon as I have.'

'That's mighty grown-up of you.' Dave looked Harlan up and down. 'I reckon you must be at least thirteen.'

Harlan puffed his chest, his throat clogging at this encouragement.

'I'm twelve come the fall.'

Dave reached into his pocket and extracted a coin.

'Then a grown-up boy who's my kin deserves something.'

Harlan held out his hand. Then his pa's warning battered at his thoughts and he withdrew his hand, but curiosity tugged at him and he held out his hand again.

With a slow wink, Dave placed the coin in the centre of his palm.

Harlan turned the coin over, his own surprise clogging his throat and silencing him a moment.

'A whole dollar!' Harlan grinned. 'And I can keep it?'

'Yup. It's yours to do with as you please.' Dave smiled and rolled on to his haunches. 'So, what are you going to do with it?'

'Don't rightly know. Never had money before.' Harlan threw the coin from hand to hand, then wrapped his fingers around it and held his chin aloft. 'But I'll listen to your advice.'

'I ain't the best person to offer advice.' Dave shrugged. 'But as you're a sensible kid, I reckon you ought to invest it.'

'What does that mean?'

'It means you don't spend it now, but store the money away.'

Harlan unclasped his fingers and stared down at the shining coin. 'I don't like the sound of that.'

'I agree, but grown-up sensible kids invest their money. And one day a dollar becomes two dollars, then three. So when they do know what they want to spend it on, they have more money to do that spending.'

'You've convinced me.' Harlan narrowed his eyes.

'How do I invest it?'

'Where's your hiding-place where you keep the secret things you don't want your parents to find?'

'Ain't got one of those.'

Dave blew out his cheeks, then edged to Harlan's side.

'Grown-up boy like you needs a place – like in a burrow, or under a stone.' Dave clamped a hand on Harlan's shoulder and turned him to face the barn doorway. 'Some place only you know about.'

As he ran this new idea around his mind, Harlan glanced through the barn doorway and within seconds a hiding-place came to mind: an abandoned burrow under the horse trough.

'I reckon I know a place.'

'Good. Then hide your dollar there and don't look at it until you need it. And when you look again, it'll have grown.'

Harlan shuffled the coin deeper into his hand and wrapped his fingers around it.

'I'll do that.'

Dave patted Harlan's shoulder, then picked up the plate and rested it on his lap.

'Now go. Your pa said you shouldn't speak to me and he'll know you have if you stay any longer.'

Harlan edged back a pace. 'How did you know that?'

'I just do.' Dave pointed at the door and winked. ' 'Bye, nephew.'

' 'Bye, uncle.' Harlan smiled, then scampered back to the house.

CHAPTER 4

'I'll be gone for a day this time,' Rourke said, 'but I should be back by sundown tomorrow.'

Celeste fingered the bowl Harlan had just retrieved from the barn. It was so clean Dave must have licked it clean after eating his breakfast.

'Be careful,' she said.

She met Rourke's gaze a moment, then lowered her head.

Rourke knew the question she wanted to ask, but he firmed his jaw, avoiding making it easy for her.

'So, I'll be going.' Rourke backed a pace towards the door.

'Rourke.' She coughed and raised her head. 'Dave was checking his rigging earlier and from the look of it, he's set to move on, but maybe if he stayed a day or two more, you might put aside your differences.'

Rourke snorted. 'You're assuming I want to put aside our differences.'

'You might not want to.' She paced across the room and laid a hand on Rourke's shoulder. 'But you should still do it.'

Rourke sighed. He glanced through the window at the barn, then patted her hand.

'All right. I'll see what he has to say for himself.'

They shared a brushed kiss and a momentary hug. Then he headed outside and to the barn.

Dave was leaning against the doorframe, whittling. He glanced up and smiled as Rourke swung to a halt to stand before him.

'Where you heading on to?' Rourke asked.

'Lincoln, then Denver.'

Rourke nodded. He half-turned away, then took a deep breath and turned back.

'I'll be gone for a day,' he murmured, staring at his feet.

'Where you heading?'

'I'm staking out in Snakepass Gully.' Rourke gulped and took another breath, then looked up. 'But if you're minded, I wouldn't complain if I found that you were still here when I return.'

Dave jutted his jaw as he nodded. 'Being as it's you that asked, brother, suppose I could postpone my business a while longer.'

Rourke waggled a firm finger at Dave. 'But if you stay, we ain't got time or money to feed you. You'll earn your keep.'

'That's the basis I always use. What you got in mind?'

Rourke shepherded Dave around to look away from the house. He pointed at the fence that was more gaps than wood some fifty yards away.

'The fence that borders Walt Silt's land is my responsibility. It needs replacing. I got the timber last year, but I ain't had time to use it.'

Dave rubbed his jaw, then nodded, so Rourke turned and headed for his horse.

Dave sauntered after him and when Rourke mounted his horse and swung it round, he lifted his hat.

'And while you're gone, you don't need to get people to look in on me. I won't cause no mischief here.'

'Can you blame me after finding you drunk and fighting in the Golden Star?'

'I can't. But I only get into trouble when I'm near a saloon or Barton May. You can trust me when I'm on our land.'

'My land,' Rourke murmured. He nodded and shook the reins. 'I'll trust you.'

'Obliged. And I also ain't looking to outstay my welcome.'

Rourke kept his jaw firm as he rode the first twenty yards, then shrugged and hurried on.

'You already have,' he whispered under his breath.

Rourke aimed his rifle at the approaching left-hand rider.

'Are you sure these men are up to no good?' Irwin asked.

For the last six hours Rourke and Irwin had staked out Snakepass Gully and again they had seen nobody – until now.

Rourke shrugged. 'Nope. But I reckon as there's only one way we can know for sure.'

Irwin nodded and aimed his rifle at the right-hand

rider. He cleared his throat.

'You men,' he shouted, the sound echoing down the gully. 'Put your hands high.'

Down in the gully the two riders flinched and looked around them. They were rough-clad and dirty, but they kept their hands on their reins and away from their holsters.

'We ain't trouble,' one of the men shouted. 'And we ain't got nothing to steal.'

'And we ain't trouble either. I'm Deputy Irwin Francis and Sheriff Rourke Bowman is beside me. We just want to ask you some questions.'

'Ask away.'

'Where are you heading?'

'That a-way.' The man pointed down the gully.

'Clever answers ain't making us feel friendly towards you. Your next answer had better be a good one or you're coming with us to Stone Creek.'

'That's mighty tough treatment for two men who ain't caused one ounce of trouble in their lives.'

'It ain't when Quinn Mendosa's gun-runners are around.'

'They're near here?' The two men glanced at each other, then edged their horses a pace down the gully. 'If Mendosa is close, we ain't talking with you all day.'

Irwin sighed and glanced at Rourke.

'What you reckon?' he said, lowering his voice. 'Question them some more or let them go?'

'They don't seem like trouble.' Rourke raised his eyebrows as he rubbed the dust from his elbows. 'But we've gained nothing for our time spent sitting here. Let's shake them and see what falls out.'

Irwin grinned his agreement and turned to face down the gully.

'Stay where you are,' he shouted and stood. 'We're coming down.'

'Ain't no need,' the man shouted. 'We just want to be on our way.'

Rourke stood too and paced over the rock before him.

'Yeah,' he shouted. 'And the sooner we get down there and talk, the sooner you'll be on your way.'

The men glared up at them. Then, with reluctant nods, they beckoned them down.

Together, Rourke and Irwin picked a route down the side of the gully. Then, leaning back, they scuffed their feet through the loose stones as, one careful pace at a time, they edged their way down.

They made slow progress and, as Irwin rounded a large boulder, his boot skidded on a heap of stones. He fell on his side and skidded five yards before his floundering arms halted him.

Rourke shuffled to Irwin's side and reached down to pull him to his feet.

With embarrassment reddening his face, Irwin nodded his thanks, then glanced down the gully.

The two men at the gully bottom had taken advantage of the distraction and were galloping away.

Irwin grunted his irritation and raised his rifle, but Rourke judged that the men were already too far away. He slammed a hand on the barrel and lowered it.

Irwin still glared at the backs of the fleeing riders a moment, then turned and scurried back up the gully towards their horses.

'At least we learned one thing,' Rourke said, hurrying to catch him. 'Those men *are* up to no good.'

CHAPTER 5

While the other children ate their dinner at school, Harlan Bowman dawdled down the trail towards his home, munching on his heel of bread.

His mother worked in Stone Creek during the day and she didn't approve of him returning home, but after his fight with Otto Fein, he decided that being elsewhere for an hour would avoid him losing even more face in front of Millicent Lester.

With his head down, he kicked stones. This hurt his bare feet, but it took his mind off his throbbing shoulder and the bruise he felt emerging on his chin.

On the edge of their land, he stopped.

Dave was leaning against a new corner fence-post, whittling. Ten new fence-posts stretched away behind him, and beyond that, Barton May was digging a hole for the next post.

From under a lowered hat, Dave looked up and smiled. He swung the knife into the back of his hand and slipped it into his pocket.

'Howdy, nephew,' he said.

Harlan nodded and wandered to his side.

'Howdy, uncle.' He pointed over Dave's shoulder at Barton. 'Why is Barton May working here?'

'He's helping me build a fence for your pa.'

'Looks to me like Barton's doing all the work.'

Dave glanced over his shoulder at Barton and chuckled.

'You know what, nephew? It looks like he is at that.'

'Pa won't like Barton working on our land.' Harlan lowered his voice. 'He doesn't like him.'

'To be honest that makes two of us.' Dave winked and leaned back against the post.

Harlan expected Dave to dismiss Barton, but Dave just smiled. Then his eyes narrowed as his gaze left Harlan's eyes.

Harlan's cheeks burned and in a self-conscious gesture he covered his bruised chin with his right hand.

'That's nothing.'

Dave pushed from his post and grabbed Harlan's hand. He lifted it and stared at his chin, then prodded around the soreness.

'That hurt?'

'Not much,' Harlan grunted. He gritted his teeth to avoid wincing.

Dave ceased his prodding and stood back, but he clamped a hand on Harlan's sore shoulder.

'And what about that? Does that hurt?'

'Perhaps a bit,' Harlan whimpered, blinking back an unbidden tear.

'I reckon you're trying to be brave, but either way, you got bruised and your pa won't be happy with that.'

'He won't mind when I tell him what happened.' Harlan shrugged from Dave's grip and puffed his chest. 'I got hurt fighting Otto Fein.'

'Truth won't help you, nephew. If I were you, I'd think up a good lie, or perhaps just a simple one like . . .' Dave shrugged, '. . . you fell over.'

'I ain't doing that. Pa told me to fight him. Otto has been taunting me for weeks.'

Dave blew out his cheeks and tipped back his hat.

'And how many bruises has this Otto got?'

'None. But that ain't important. I showed him he can't taunt me.'

'Yeah, but taunting doesn't bruise you.' Dave leaned down and placed his hands on his knees. 'So what happens when Otto taunts you again?'

'I'll fight him again and I'll keep on fighting him until I win.' Harlan clenched a fist, then winced and rubbed his shoulder. 'Although I might wait a day or two until it don't hurt so much to fight.'

Dave's smile widened as he contemplated Harlan.

Harlan detected something in Dave's eyes. He guessed it was bemusement and not admiration.

Dave straightened. 'Am I right in thinking that this Otto is bigger and older than you are?'

'Yup.'

'Then I can't see you beating him for a while yet, unless you get a whole lot better at fighting real quick.'

'That ain't as important as facing up to bullies.' Harlan clenched his other fist. 'A man has to stand up for himself.'

'I always thought it was more important to win.'

Dave extracted his knife from his pocket and

returned to his whittling.

Harlan glanced at Barton, who had now righted a pole in the latest hole and had moved on to digging the next hole.

He sauntered a few paces towards the house, but Dave's final comment battered at his thoughts and his shoulder throbbed so he stopped, then shuffled back to Dave.

'I've been thinking and I reckon you could be right. Winning might be less painful than losing.' Harlan shuffled a pace closer to Dave. 'Do you know how I might win?'

Dave nodded. 'I do. Who's the biggest boy in school?'

'Otto Fein.'

'Then who's the second biggest?'

Rourke and Irwin crested the top of the gully, mounted their horses, then galloped along the flat mesa top for around 400 yards as they headed after the two fleeing men.

Single file, they edged down a dry water channel until they reached the end of the steepest part of the gully, which was still one hundred feet above ground level.

By this time, the men were already a good 500 yards ahead. But both Irwin and Rourke knew this gully well and the usual trail was winding ahead, so instead, they kept high. Although the loose rock made the route slippery, their sure-footed horses could more than make up their quarries' apparent advantage and close the gap more directly.

Sure enough, by the time they were half-way along the snaking section of the gully, they were only one hundred yards behind them. Here, they split, Rourke heading to the gully bottom and Irwin continuing on the more direct route.

Both quarries glanced back frequently, but neither fired at Rourke.

With Rourke's greater knowledge of the trail, he slowed in the right places and sped where needed and at each corner he'd gained on the riders.

Both men were also riding with different levels of skill, and as Rourke closed, they glanced over their shoulders, shared a short barked argument, then separated. One man hurried on ahead leaving the other man, who was faring less well, to make his own slower progress.

Within another half-mile, a 200-yard gap had opened up between the fleeing men and Rourke was only fifty yards behind the trailing man.

Then Irwin emerged from his different route on to the trail between the two riders.

The trailing rider flinched and pulled back on the reins, causing his horse to rear. Caught in a moment of indecision, he swung his horse round in all directions, but only succeeded in throwing himself to the ground.

Irwin glanced left and right. Then, with a slap of his hand against his thigh, he relented in his pursuit of the other man and hurried back towards the fallen rider, who was now scrambling on hands and feet through the sagebrush until he reached a tangle of boulders.

Both lawmen dismounted and dashed for cover on either side of him.

'You ain't going anywhere,' Rourke shouted as he gained cover. 'It's time to give yourself up.'

'I ain't done anything wrong,' the man shouted from behind his covering boulder.

'For a man who ain't done anything wrong, you were riding from the law pretty damn fast.' Rourke sighed. 'But if you're innocent, you got nothing to worry about and you can be on your way.'

The man leapt up from behind the boulder.

'You ain't taking me,' he shouted and blasted a shot at Rourke. The lead cannoned into the ground ten feet before Rourke, but Rourke still ducked.

On his knees, he shuffled round the side of the boulder until he could see Irwin, who was hiding beside another rock thirty yards away. The two men exchanged hand-signals, after which Irwin ducked from view.

'That just wasn't wise,' Rourke shouted.

'Maybe not, but I don't know you. You could be Quinn Mendosa for all I know and I ain't falling into his hands.'

'I ain't Quinn Mendosa. I'm Sheriff Rourke Bowman and I just want to ask you some questions.'

'Prove it.'

'I will. I'm standing now and walking towards you.' Rourke stood, unfolding his legs with steady care. 'If you fire at me again, you'll either die here today or swing later. But if you back down, we can sort this out.'

Rourke kept his gun drawn, but held it down as he

paced out from his cover. Ten yards before him, only the top of the man's hat was visible above the boulder.

With slow, long paces, Rourke stalked towards the boulder. Ten paces before it, he swung to a halt.

The man glanced up, then hid again,

'I can see you got a star.'

For long moments Rourke stood hunched and waiting. Then the man stood. With nervous glances in all directions, the man paced out from the boulder and stood before it with his gun pointing down.

Behind him a flurry of motion blurred to disappear behind the rock the man was previously hiding behind, but Rourke kept his gaze on the man.

'You're acting real sensible so far. Let's see if you can keep it up. Throw down your gun and we can talk.'

The man glanced at his gun, then twitched, but as he lifted the gun, Irwin leapt out from behind the rock and rammed into the man's back, bundling him to the ground. They rolled over each other before Irwin thrust the man's shoulders to the ground, pinning him down, by which time Rourke had scurried towards them and kicked the man's gun away.

Irwin lifted on his haunches, rolled the man on to his front, and pulled his hands behind his back.

'I wasn't going to fire,' the man whined, craning his neck up to see Rourke, his eyes wide and scared. 'I was just throwing down my gun like you said.'

'Perhaps you were, or perhaps you weren't,' Rourke said. 'But as I ain't sure, you're returning to Stone Creek to answer some questions.'

The man grinned. 'And then can I go?'

Rourke dragged the man to his feet and pushed him forward a pace.

'That depends on whether we like your answers.'

CHAPTER 6

When Rourke and Irwin returned to Stone Creek, they questioned their prisoner, but his former promises of good faith disappeared and a surly obstinacy prevailed as he refused to divulge even his name or provide any details of what he was doing or where he was going.

Blank-faced silence greeted all their questions on whether he was a member of Mendosa's gun-runners.

If Rourke weren't searching for Quinn Mendosa, he'd have had no choice but to release his prisoner, but he decided his actions were sufficiently suspect to detain him awhile. So he locked him in a cell, after which Irwin volunteered to sleep in the office for the night to enable Rourke to return home.

Rourke didn't complain.

Twilight was reddening the horizon when he rode down the trail towards his home.

On the edge of his land, he stopped a moment. A part of him was looking forward to his unexpected early arrival catching Dave off-guard. He was sure that Dave would have failed to do the work he'd given him, but to his surprise, a row of fence-posts stretched for thirty yards beyond the edge of the trail and scuffed earth beyond marked out the direction of the remaining fence.

For a day's work this was an average showing, but it was far better than he'd expected from Dave.

He dismounted and patted the nearest post, finding it solid. Whistling to himself, he paced to his house, tethered his horse, and dashed inside.

'You're early,' Celeste said, frowning.

Rourke ignored Celeste's unenthusiastic reception and shared a long hug with her, then stepped back.

'I reckon we might have captured one of Mendosa's gun-runners and . . . ' Rourke considered Celeste's furrowed brow. 'What's wrong? It ain't Dave, is it, because I was all set to congratulate him on erecting so many posts?'

'It isn't Dave. It's Harlan.' She sighed. 'Miss Wainwright says he got into another fight at school.'

Rourke glanced at Harlan's closed door. 'How bad is he hurt?'

'Aside from some bruising, he isn't hurt that much. But Otto Fein has a broken arm.'

Rourke winced. 'Can't say that boy doesn't deserve it.'

'I agree. But that isn't why I'm punishing Harlan.' She took a deep breath and looked away from Rourke. 'He lied about the incident.'

Rourke snorted, considering Celeste for long moments until she looked at him. Still he stared at her another ten seconds, forcing his anger to subside so that he could order his thoughts.

'Harlan!' he roared. 'Get out here.'

He turned to face Harlan's door and folded his arms. At his side, Celeste matched his posture.

In a strange way admonishing Harlan was a task he usually enjoyed. It proved to him that he could resolve domestic problems without need of the beatings to which his father had always resorted.

But if there was one thing that tested that resolve to the limit, it was the possibility of Harlan being dishonest.

An inch at a time Harlan's door squeaked open and Harlan shuffled through with his head down. He looked up, met Rourke's gaze for the barest moment with his own watery gaze, then hung his head again.

'I'm sorry, Pa,' he said, his voice a croaked whisper.

Rourke breathed deeply before he trusted himself to speak.

'I've told you, boy. I will never punish you like my pa punished me. You get into as many fights as you need to – provided you don't start them. But the day you start lying is the day I start using my belt.'

'But I didn't lie,' Harlan whined.

Rourke glanced at Celeste. She returned a slow shake of her head, then returned to staring down at Harlan.

'If you say that you didn't lie, I believe you. So just tell me what happened.'

Harlan scuffed his bare foot in a circle, then looked up, his face reddening with each heartbeat.

'I don't reckon you want . . .' Harlan gulped as Rourke flared his eyes.

'Just take a deep breath, boy, and tell me everything.'

Harlan took a deep breath, gulped again, then took another breath.

'Otto Fein and Torn Longhorn got into a fight,' Harlan babbled, 'when he got it into his head that he'd stolen his jacket and the fight got going something fearsome and he knocked him over a fence and he came back at him all angry-like and he pushed and shoved and the fight got closer to the creek and I don't reckon he meant to cause him that much pain but he fell in the creek and when he came up his arm was all bent and he was crying and Doc Simpson had to put something over his mouth to stop him wailing and Miss Wainwright sent us home early and well, that's it.'

Rourke sighed. 'I ain't sure I understood all that, but are you saying that you weren't involved?'

'I wasn't.'

'And the bruise on your chin?'

'That was something else.'

Rourke glanced at Celeste and raised his eyebrows.

'So,' she said, 'tell your pa why Miss Wainwright let all the other children go home on their own, but she escorted you into town.'

Harlan lowered his head even further until Rourke could see the back of his reddened neck.

'She reckoned I put Torn up to hurting Otto.'

'And did you?' Rourke asked.

'I didn't.'

Celeste turned to Rourke. 'So there it is. Either

42

Miss Wainwright got it wrong or Harlan is lying.'

Celeste stood shoulder to shoulder with Rourke and they stared down at the boy with their arms folded and each tapping a foot on the floor.

Harlan edged from foot to foot and glanced around the room, his face glowing even redder with each repeated gulp.

Rourke was pleased that Harlan was so bad at lying that he was being obvious in his efforts to hide his lie, and in other circumstances he'd have let amusement get the better of him, but he still glared down at him, waiting until their disapproving silence broke him.

'I wasn't lying,' Harlan whispered. 'But I *did* tell Torn that Otto had stolen his jacket, even though I hid it.'

'And why ain't that lying?'

'Because it wasn't my idea to tell him that, so I wasn't lying – as such.'

Rourke narrowed his eyes. 'You're treading a fine line with the truth, boy. Whose idea was it?'

Harlan looked up, his eyes tearful and pleading.

'I promised I wouldn't tell whose idea it was and telling will break that promise and I can't do that.'

'Then it looks to me like you got yourself a problem.' Rourke tipped back his hat and leaned down to place his hands on his knees so that he shared Harlan's eye-line. 'You either take the belt for lying, or prove you didn't lie by telling me who gave you the idea.'

Harlan glanced at Rourke's belt, but then shook his head and looked up.

'I can't tell. I promised.'

Rourke stood tall as Harlan hung his head again. He glanced at Celeste, who gave the slightest shake of her head. Rourke sighed, pleased that he didn't have to beat Harlan, but still wanting him to prove that he was telling the truth.

As he searched for a solution, he glanced away from Harlan and through the window. His gaze fell on the barn. His eyes narrowed.

'Harlan!' he roared.

Harlan flinched and looked up. 'Yes?'

'Are you refusing to tell me whose fault it was because you disobeyed my order not to talk to Dave and he told you to set Torn on Otto?'

Harlan winced and shuffled back a pace.

Celeste caught Rourke's eye and nodded.

'Harlan,' she whispered, 'go to your room.'

Harlan rocked back on forth on his heels, then scurried to his room and slammed the door shut.

'Dave,' Rourke murmured. 'I knew he'd cause trouble before too long.'

'Perhaps.' Celeste shook her head. 'But one of the other boys still might have given Harlan the idea.'

'They wouldn't. They're all decent boys at heart, even Torn and Otto, but that don't go for Dave.'

She shrugged, then snorted a harsh chuckle.

'But at least that fence looks fine.'

Rourke rolled his shoulders and turned to the door.

'That won't stop me kicking him off my land.'

Celeste laid a hand on Rourke's arm.

'Rourke, don't say anything you might regret later. Dave's still your kin, and if it was him, I reckon he had Harlan's interest in mind, even if it was misguided.'

Rourke sneered. He shrugged from Celeste's hand and headed outside. With his head down, he stormed straight to the barn. He stamped his feet as he stopped and stood with his hands on his hips before the doorway.

'Dave!' he roared. 'Come out, *now*.'

For long moments he waited, but Dave didn't appear. He glanced over his shoulder as Celeste emerged from the house.

'He was here when I got home,' she said, joining him.

'Come out, you ugly varmint!' Rourke roared.

Shuffling sounded in the barn, but when a man edged into the doorway it was Barton May.

'Dave ain't here,' he murmured. 'He headed into town.'

'Forget Dave,' Rourke snapped. 'What in tarnation are you doing here?'

Barton hunched his shoulders and rubbed a hand over his bristled cheeks.

'I kind of helped Dave with your fence and in return Dave said I could spend a night or two in here and share his dinner.' Barton smiled.

'Are you really so stupid that you think I'll let you sleep in my...' Rourke hung his head a moment and sighed. 'How much of my fence did you build?'

'I helped.' Barton considered Rourke's firm-jawed gaze. 'I did it all.'

Rourke glanced away, shaking his head, then turned back to Barton.

'Suppose if a Bowman family member offered you a deal and you fulfilled your side of it, I should honour that promise.' He glanced at Celeste. 'Give him Dave's dinner. And after he's spent a night in the barn, he can eat Dave's breakfast tomorrow.'

'Obliged,' Barton said, grinning. 'And if you're pleased with my work, I'd be minded to finish that fence in return for a few more meals.'

Rourke pointed a firm finger at Barton. 'Don't push your luck.'

As Barton shuffled back into the barn, Rourke headed to his horse and mounted it.

'Rourke,' Celeste called after him. 'Don't do anything you'll regret later.'

Rourke snorted and urged his horse to gallop from his house.

CHAPTER 7

When Rourke rode into Stone Creek, he tethered his horse outside the sheriff's office, then strode straight to the Golden Star. Dave's horse wasn't outside, but it was further down the road outside the Lucky Dip.

Rourke headed to the saloon and pushed open the doors. He hung on to them a moment as he glanced around the room.

In the half-filled saloon, Dave was propped against the bar, and from his slouched posture over his whiskey-glass and the low level of the whiskey in the bottle before him, he'd probably been here for some time.

Rourke took a deep breath, then paced to Dave's side and leaned on the bar at his side.

From the corner of his eye Dave glanced his way, flinched, then stood tall.

'Howdy, brother,' he said. His voice was slurred, but not as badly as it had been two nights ago.

Rourke forced himself to smile. 'Howdy to you. Thought I'd find you in one of Stone Creek's saloons.'

'Well, after Barton May broke that window in the Golden Star, I ain't welcome there, so I had no choice of saloons.'

'You broke that . . .' Rourke hung his head a moment, then considered Dave. 'You celebrating your first ever day of honest work?'

'It ain't my first.' Dave flicked up the corners of his mouth with a slight smile. 'Is that your way of saying I did a good job with the fence?'

'The man who built my fence did a good job, and I can't say that I ain't surprised.'

Dave bit his bottom lip, then hunched over his drink.

'Glad to hear it.'

Rourke grabbed Dave's shoulder and spun him round to face him.

'And even when I gave you the chance, you still didn't tell me that Barton May built my fence and not you.'

Dave shrugged away from Rourke's hand.

'Does it matter?'

'It does. I didn't give you that job because it needed doing just now. I gave it to you so that you could prove to me that you ain't the useless heap of saloon trash I reckoned you were.'

'You smug varmint.' Dave grabbed his glass and slammed it on the bar, splashing the whiskey over his hand. 'I ain't got to prove anything to you.'

'When a lawman has an outlaw for a brother, that outlaw has to do a mighty lot of proving.'

Dave swung round and shook the glass in Rourke's face.

'I ain't no outlaw.'

Rourke snorted. 'So you spent time in Leavenworth jail as a guard, did you?'

Dave glared back at Rourke, then turned and hunched over the bar.

'I've done a few things I ain't proud of, but they were brought on by hunger, not greed.'

'It's always the same with you – nothing is ever your fault and you always take the easy route.'

'Perhaps you're right, but hard work gets you nowhere.' Dave tapped his forehead. 'Thinking does. And I got Barton to build your fence using some mighty fine bargaining.'

'My family don't need the kind of help your bargaining might get us.'

Dave shrugged, then grabbed the whiskey-bottle from the bar and poured himself a generous measure.

'Quit whining, brother. Ain't no need to get all flustered about a fence. You wanted it built. It's half-built. And Barton will finish it in another day or so – under my supervision.'

'I'm not whining about the fence. I'm whining about your low-down ways: ways that don't sort out your own problems, ways that avoid facing the results of your actions, ways that make other people suffer from your behaviour.'

'I ain't sure what you mean.' Dave narrowed his eyes. 'What you digging up from our past?'

'Nothing. I keep on giving you a chance to volunteer information before I have to drag it out of you, but you keep on ignoring that chance.' Rourke slammed his hands on his hips and leaned down to thrust his face inches from Dave's face. 'So, what advice have you given Harlan?'

'Ah, that.' Dave shrugged and edged back a pace. 'I thought you'd be pleased.'

'Otto Fein got himself a broken arm.'

'Better another boy than Harlan.'

'Nobody had to get a broken arm.'

Dave fingered his whiskey-glass, then placed it on the bar and faced up to Rourke.

'Harlan was getting all messed up following your advice of standing up for himself. I just showed him another way.'

'You did. You showed him your way, and your way ain't the way I want him to know about.'

Dave lifted on his heels and glared into Rourke's eyes, but then blinked and looked away. His shoulders slumped and he backed a pace with his hands raised.

'You're right, brother,' he murmured. 'I'm sorry.'

With this sudden back-down, Rourke sighed and lowered his head.

'I accept your apology.'

Dave chuckled and leaned on the bar.

'Next time, I'll let him get all messed up and not help.'

'There ain't no next time.'

Dave ran a finger around the top of his glass.

'That mean you're running me off your land?'

'No. You ain't even there for me to run you off. Barton May is in your place and that's a big improvement on who slept in the barn last night.' Rourke looked Dave up and down. 'As far as I'm concerned, you're just some trash littering up the saloon.'

Rourke turned away, but Dave grabbed his arm and swung him back.

'You can tell me I was wrong to interfere in the way you bring up your son. You can criticize me for the way I got your work done. You can run me off your land. But you ain't walking away from me after dismissing me as some piece of saloon trash.'

Rourke snorted and stood toe to toe with Dave. He looked him straight in the eye.

'You're trash, Dave. You always have been and you always will be. The only thing worse than having you as my kin is knowing that every day you're alive, you're ruining our good family name.'

Dave glared at Rourke, then shook his head. With one finger, he lifted his hat a mite, then moved to lean on the bar.

Without warning, he swung back and hurled a backhanded slap at Rourke's face, but Rourke thrust up an arm, knocking it away, then danced back a pace.

Dave raised both his fists as he backed two paces.

'Come on,' he muttered, 'put your fists up.'

'I ain't.' Rourke raised his hands with the palms facing Dave. 'And put those fists down. Hitting a lawman is a mighty serious offence.'

'I ain't looking to hit no lawman, just my smug, opinionated brother, who I reckon is long overdue a good thrashing.'

For long moments Rourke glared at Dave, but then with a slow nod, he bunched his fists. Still, he kept them held low as the two men circled each other with their gazes set on each other's eyes.

The other saloon folk backed away, leaving a clear space before the bar.

Dave rolled his shoulders, then weighed in with a flurry of blows, but Rourke weaved and ducked away from most of them, only the occasional glancing blow hitting him.

Dave relented and took a deep breath.

'You fought your anger out?' Rourke muttered.

'Quit talking and fight.'

'I ain't fighting with you.' Rourke snorted. 'You ain't worth it.'

Dave uttered a short oath and stormed in. He threw back his fist and aimed it in a solid slug at Rourke's face.

Again Rourke ducked, the blow whistling over his head, but Dave swung up with his left fist.

Rourke rocked back and the blow thrust past his shoulder, but the force of the missed blow made Dave stagger forward and tumble into Rourke. With a mixture of elbows, forearms and fists, he pummelled Rourke's chest. From so close his berserk blows landed with little force and Rourke merely shrugged them off, then stood tall and pushed Dave away.

'Fight, damn you,' Dave muttered as he gained his footing.

'I'm a lawman. I don't brawl with saloon trash.' Rourke smirked as he met Dave's eye. 'But if you land a real punch on me, I will arrest this piece of saloon trash.'

Dave raised his fists and strode towards Rourke, his stance wide.

'I don't need your pathetic taunts to rile me. I've already got enough reasons to knock that smug grin off your face.'

Rourke backed and pace by pace they edged towards the saloon doors, but at the doors Rourke circled around and back into the saloon.

Dave halted and as Rourke wandered by him, he leapt at Rourke, pushing him back against a table. Then, as the table creaked, he grabbed his jacket and tried to hurl him backwards over it.

Rourke leaned back and set his legs wide, resisting Dave's efforts, but Dave grabbed a firmer grip of his jacket and tried to wrestle him to the floor. Again Rourke stood firm, but then their combined weight collapsed the table and they tumbled to the floor in a tangle of splintered wood.

Rourke landed heavily over a broken table-leg with Dave on top of him. Momentarily winded, he could only shake his head as Dave rolled to his haunches and dragged him up with one hand, then slugged his jaw with the other hand.

The blow knocked Rourke on his side and he lay a moment, trying to maintain the even temper that had overcome him the moment he'd walked into the saloon, but with his jaw throbbing, he leapt to his feet and raised his fists.

'I reckon,' he muttered, 'that punch was good enough for me to arrest you.'

Dave grinned. 'I'm glad you're riled too. Reckon I can enjoy myself now.'

Rourke snorted and advanced a long pace on Dave, but Dave stood his ground and hurled a punch at Rourke's face. The blow smashed into Rourke's cheek, but Rourke shrugged it off and threw all his strength into one long, round-armed punch to Dave's body. The blow landed with solid force. His fist buried itself deep into Dave's guts.

Bent double Dave staggered back and around, gasping for air. With his body unguarded, Rourke threw another solid punch to Dave's jaw which wheeled him to the floor. As Dave skidded to a halt, Rourke flexed his hand, finding the knuckles numb but undamaged.

With his fists lowered, he stood over Dave.

'Get up, you piece of trash,' he muttered. 'You're littering up the saloon again.'

With his eyes blazing, Dave staggered to his feet and wheeled back two paces before he regained his footing, then straightened and raised his fists, but slower than before.

'Quit talking, brother,' he grunted, 'and start fighting.'

Dave lurched forward, then broke into a run with his arms wide, aiming to bundle Rourke to the floor, but Rourke danced to the side and as Dave trundled past him, he helped him on his way with a firm kick to the rear.

Dave stumbled to his knees, cracking his head against the side of the bar. With a whining groan, he crumpled to lie on his back. His head lolled.

Rourke stalked round Dave's body and stared down at him, but as only the first dark hints of an ugly bruise were emerging on Dave's forehead and not blood, he grabbed his legs behind the knees, then dragged him backwards, ensuring Dave slid over the roughest length of floor.

The bartender edged out from behind the bar to help him, but Rourke shook his head. He speeded his pacing and, as he dragged Dave through the door, Dave's head rocked up and down, thudding heavily at least three times.

Outside, Rourke maintained a firm pace, ensuring he walked over every length of rotten board, only relenting to fetch Irwin's help when he reached the sheriff's office.

Then, with Irwin's help, he carried Dave into the office and threw him in the endmost cell.

'What's the charge?' Irwin asked.

'Fighting in the saloon.' Rourke batted his hands free of dust, then rubbed his cheek. 'And punching a lawman.'

Irwin slammed the cell door closed. 'And what do I do with him?'

'Let him sleep it off. Then at sun-up tomorrow, run him out of town.'

Irwin nodded and turned to Rourke. 'I'll wait until you get here.'

'Don't bother.' Rourke glanced at the comatose Dave and snorted. 'When I get here in the morning, I want him to be long gone.'

CHAPTER 8

At sun-up Rourke awoke. Without saying a word to Celeste he dressed and wandered outside.

With his sullen mood furrowing his brow, he stalked around the edge of his land and watched the sun burn away a low mist that was blanketing the ground. At each new fence-post, he stopped and patted the wood, but they were all as solid as they looked.

This discovery didn't soothe his irritation, but on the way back to his house, he checked on Barton. Although he hadn't planned to, in a magnanimous gesture he told Barton that he could stay in the barn until he'd finished the fence.

He watched Barton scurry away to begin work, even before breakfast, and for a fleeting moment Rourke wished that if he had to have a worthless brother, he could be as worthless as Barton was.

Then he shivered, dismissing this thought, and returned to his house.

Celeste gave him space for his brooding and, however he looked at his situation, going into Stone

Creek to see Dave before Irwin ran him out of town would only generate another fruitless argument. So he sat at the table and watched the sun inch above the horizon as he ensured that it'd be too late to see Dave when he headed into town.

Two hours into the morning, Celeste beckoned him to the window and for the first time today he was smiling as he looked outside. The smile died.

Riding down the trail was Irwin, and in his tow was Dave.

As Rourke muttered to himself, Celeste bustled Harlan into his room, then, with just a glance, beseeched Rourke to use this situation.

And with just a return glance, Rourke refused her offer.

As Celeste followed Harlan into his room, Rourke sat at the table and tapped his fingers on the wood until Irwin entered the house with Dave shuffling on behind.

'Let's hear it,' he murmured, his voice calm as he glared at Irwin.

Irwin pulled out a chair and sat, but Dave remained standing.

'It's about that man we arrested yesterday,' Irwin said. He glanced at Dave, who leaned down on the table.

'I recognized him,' Dave said.

Rourke snorted. 'I expect you would. Worthless outlaws tend to know each other. What of it?'

Dave pushed back from the table and glanced away, muttering to himself, then turned back.

'Because,' he snapped, 'if you stopped looking for

the worst in me, brother, you might learn something to your advantage.'

'Then teach me something.' Rourke held his hands wide. 'There's a first time for everything.'

Dave took a deep breath. 'The man is Tanner Eldridge. I met him some years back.'

'In jail I assume.'

'Yeah.'

'And?'

'And he's told you nothing, and unless you get something on him real quick, you'll have to release him, but if I were to talk to him, he might tell me things he'd never tell you.' Dave raised his eyebrows. 'And that might include information about gun-runners and a man called Quinn Mendosa.'

Rourke snorted. 'And I suppose in return I'll have to let you fester away for another night in my barn? And after that, you'll find another way to wangle another night, and then—'

'No!' Dave slammed his fist on the table. 'I ain't staying another night in your pathetic, rat-infested barn.'

'Good. Because Barton May is staying there and you know what?' Rourke leaned back in his chair and smiled. 'I'm already starting to think of him as a member of my family.'

Dave snorted and turned to glare through the window.

Irwin glanced at Rourke, shaking his head.

'Rourke,' he said, 'just listen to what Dave's offering.'

Rourke winced, then leaned on the table and massaged his eyes.

'I'll listen, but only when Dave tells me what he hopes to gain from volunteering this information.'

Dave turned, his upper lip curled in a sneer.

'I can only keep on saying this: as soon as I can, I'm heading to Denver to get myself some worthwhile company, but before I leave, I just reckoned I might help my only brother.'

Rourke glared at Dave, but as Dave returned an equally firm glare, he glanced at Irwin to find his deputy smiling at him and nodding.

Rourke sighed. 'Wait here. I'll discuss this with Irwin.'

Rourke rose from the table and sauntered outside. Irwin murmured to Dave, but Rourke was grinding his teeth and didn't hear what he said. Midway between the barn and his house he turned and raised his eyebrows.

'I don't know whether Dave is telling the truth or not,' Irwin said, joining him. 'But I do know I want to catch Mendosa's gun-runners, and if Dave can help us, I ain't questioning his motives.'

'You're a good lawman, Irwin. But I can't look at this like you can. I reckon Dave is just trying to wheedle himself into my family.' Rourke grunted and tipped back his hat. 'And I ain't letting him do that.'

'He says he wants to leave as much as you want him to leave.'

'What Dave says and what Dave wants ain't the same.' Rourke glanced at his house where Dave was watching him through the window. 'That man has no concept of the truth other than how to avoid it.'

'I reckon you're right, but you should put your duties before your personal problems.'

For long moments Rourke glared at Irwin, but then nodded.

'I should. So what information has he got on Tanner?'

Irwin tipped back his hat and sighed.

'It might be better if he explains it to you.'

'No. It'd be better if you explained it to me.' Rourke held his hands wide. 'It's the only way you'll ensure I listen.'

'It ain't information.' Irwin edged a pace closer to Rourke. 'Dave reckons he can trick Tanner into helping us track down Mendosa.'

Rourke narrowed his eyes. 'He reckons – *what*?'

'Like I said, he'd better explain. But from the sound of it, we could capture Mendosa, and that's more than we'll do without his help.'

Rourke glanced away, whistling his breath through his nostrils, but then provided a reluctant nod.

'I'll listen.' Rourke raised a finger. 'But that's all I'm promising.'

Irwin turned and waved to the house, beckoning to Dave, who strode through the door and paced towards them, smiling.

'So,' he said, 'do you want my help or not?'

Rourke sighed and folded his arms.

'Against my better judgement,' he said, 'Irwin's persuaded me to listen to you. What's your plan?'

'I'll tell you, but I'm sure you won't like it.' Dave shrugged. 'Except for the first part, mind.'

*

With Dave's arm grasped firmly in his right hand, Irwin strode into the sheriff's office. He marched Dave to the cell beside Tanner Eldridge's cell, then unlocked the cell and thrust him inside.

'As you ain't learnt your lesson,' he muttered, locking the cell, 'you get another day in here.'

Dave glared back at Irwin, then stalked to the back of the cell and hurled himself on the bunk.

Irwin watched him a moment, then strode to his desk. When Irwin slammed his feet on the desk, Dave drew a leg up to his chin, then leaned back against the wall and pulled his hat low.

'Howdy, Dave.'

Dave shuffled down into his jacket and stared at the bars before him.

'I said,' Tanner said from the adjoining cell, 'howdy, Dave.'

Dave glanced into the empty cell to his left, then turned to the cell to his right.

'You talking to me?' he asked, staring at Tanner.

'I sure am,' Tanner said with laughter in his voice, 'Dave Bowman.'

Dave shrugged and turned his gaze to the front bars again.

'Reckon as you have the wrong man.'

'I thought I recognized your voice when that deputy kicked you out this morning, but I couldn't place you. But it is you, Dave.'

'You're mistaken.'

Tanner laughed. 'You ain't changed. You were

always avoiding trouble when we shared a cell in
Leavenworth jail.'

Dave rubbed his chin and glanced at Tanner from
the corner of his eye.

'And does this Dave Bowman owe you money?'

'Nope.'

'Then howdy to you, Tanner Eldridge.' Dave
tipped his hat, then shuffled along his bunk until he
was closer to Tanner. 'So why are you stinking up the
cell next to mine?'

'Same reason as you.' Tanner sighed. 'I got
caught.'

At midday Irwin walked across the sheriff's office to
Dave's cell. With a flick of the wrist, he unlocked the
cell.

'All right,' he said. 'You can go now.'

'Thought I had a day in here,' Dave whined.

'Then I'd have to feed you and I don't reckon you
deserve that. You have five minutes to leave town.
Then I'll be running you—'

'I understand,' Dave muttered. He swung off the
bunk and sauntered through the cell door.

He stopped a moment to glance over his shoulder
and tip his hat to Tanner, then shuffled from the
office.

Irwin glanced into Tanner's cell. 'But you are
going nowhere.'

'Quit gloating,' Tanner muttered. 'You got nothing on me. You can't hold me for ever.'

'I could fetch Marshal Devine and see if he can
make you talk.'

Tanner gulped. 'Just get me some dinner.'

Irwin shrugged. 'Being as you asked so nicely, I will.'

Irwin strode outside and walked past the office window. A dull thud sounded, then a crunch as of a heavy object falling to the ground.

Dave shuffled past the window, walking backwards and edged into the office. Dragged along behind him was Irwin's prone form.

He pulled Irwin behind the desk so that he would-n't be visible from the road, then scurried into the corner, grabbed the cell keys, and dashed to the cells. On the third try, he found which key unlocked Tanner's cell and swung it open.

Tanner patted a firm hand on Dave's back, then dashed to the desk. He removed his gun from the top drawer, then unhooked Irwin's gunbelt and held it out to Dave.

'Never had much use for a gun,' Dave said.

Tanner thrust the belt forward. 'Kind of reckon you should change your mind now that you've broken me out of here.'

Dave glanced away a moment, then nodded and grabbed the belt.

Both men stalked outside. Few people were on the road and nobody was looking their way so they calmly mounted their horses outside the office and trotted out of town, heading east. But when they were clear of the last buildings, they speeded to a gallop.

Within the office all was quiet for a minute. Then Irwin opened an eye. He rolled to his feet and crawled to the window. A peek outside confirmed that Tanner and Dave had gone.

He was just swinging a new gunbelt from the armoury around his waist when Rourke strode in.

'You ready?' Irwin asked.

'Yup,' Rourke said. 'And Dave was right about one thing. I still don't like his plan much.'

CHAPTER 9

Rourke jumped down from his horse and knelt by the trail. Scuffed earth indicated that at least one horse had headed off the trail here, but whether the riders were Dave and Tanner he couldn't tell.

For the first five miles out of town the two lawmen had followed their trail, but as neither lawman was a tracker they had lost that trail as soon as their quarries had headed off the usual route east.

He glanced up at Irwin, but Irwin returned a shrug.

'I still reckon we lost their trail two miles back,' Irwin said.

Rourke grunted his annoyance and peered into the hills, seeing no movement or any signs to suggest that Dave and Tanner had passed this way. Rourke lifted a stone that might have been disturbed in the last hour, but then again, might have been disturbed earlier.

'Dave should have kept a straight course that we could follow, or left a sign.'

'Or ridden slow enough for us to see him.' Irwin

sighed. 'But I guess he couldn't raise Tanner's suspicions. He had to appear that he was trying to throw any pursuers off his trail.'

'Yeah. He had to appear that he was trying.' Rourke hurled the stone to the ground. 'Don't mean that he had to succeed.'

Irwin tipped back his hat and hunched forward in the saddle.

'Unless we get ourselves a whole lot of luck, I suppose we have to wait until Dave contacts us.'

'We do.' Rourke stalked back to his horse and mounted it. 'And that's what's annoying me the most.'

After an hour of hard riding, followed by another hour of steady progress, Tanner and Dave rode into a small encampment.

The encampment nestled at the base of a huge overhanging crag half-way along Hard Gulch. It was set back and guarded by towering rocks on either side and, such was the sense of security that the remote position provided, only one guard was sitting at the entrance. This man nodded to Tanner, and although his eyes narrowed as he glared at Dave, he waved them through.

Before a covered wagon, seven men sat around a smouldering fire playing chuck-a-luck and gibbering their enjoyment of the simple game.

One of the men, Waldo Hood, sauntered from the game to watch them approach. He stood with his feet wide apart and his face set in what Dave took to be a permanent sneer.

Tanner took the lead. Twenty yards from the fire, he pulled up and nodded to Waldo.

'Didn't expect to see you again,' Waldo said.

'I got lucky.'

Avery Grant rolled to his feet and joined Waldo.

'That mean the lawmen had nothing on you?' he asked.

'They didn't, but they suspected plenty, so they were planning to get Marshal Devine to take me away.' Tanner glanced to the side. 'But then my old friend, Dave, got arrested too.'

Tanner glanced over his shoulder and gestured for Dave to draw alongside.

'And I broke him out of the sheriff's office,' Dave said.

'And he has plenty of other talents.' Tanner leaned forward in the saddle. 'And after what he did, I reckon they're the kind of talents we're looking for.'

Waldo sneered and spat to the side. 'We got all the talents we need.'

'That ain't your decision,' Tanner muttered. 'Mendosa decides how much help we need.'

'He does.' Waldo hooked a thumb in his gunbelt and glared up at Dave from under a lowered hat. 'But your friend only gets to see him if he impresses me.'

'All right.' Dave dismounted and strode five paces to stand before Waldo. 'Tell me what you're doing and I'll tell you how I can help.'

Waldo narrowed his eyes, then glanced at Tanner.

'I ain't told him,' Tanner said.

'You're a wise man.' Waldo strode a pace to loom over Dave. He licked his lips as he searched Dave's eyes. 'We're gun-running.'

Dave gulped and glanced away. 'I didn't realize.'

'That frighten you?'

'Suppose it does.' Dave lowered his head and scratched the back of neck.

'I don't care what he thinks,' Avery muttered. 'He ain't joining us. We got enough people now that Tanner is back. The return ain't getting any bigger and we don't need anyone else to share it.'

'I reckon that goes for me too,' Waldo muttered, then pointed at the men around the fire. 'And I reckon it's the same for everybody else.'

As muttered agreement rippled around the fire, Tanner dismounted and joined Dave, who was still shaking his head and staring at the ground.

'If Dave joins us,' Tanner said, 'he won't cut down what you'll make. He can have a quarter of my share.'

'A mighty fine offer.' Waldo glanced at Avery, who raised his eyebrows, but then gave a curt nod. He turned back to Tanner. 'But is he any good?'

'He is. I can vouch for him.'

'You already have.' Waldo forced the thinnest of smiles and turned to Dave.

Dave gulped, then raised his head to face him.

'If you've finished talking about me,' he said, 'I reckon I can speak for myself. And if it's all the same to you, I reckon as I'll leave. What you're doing might just get me killed and I ain't risking my life for a quarter share.'

'Hey,' Tanner muttered, grabbing Dave's arm. 'I risked plenty bringing you here.'

Dave ripped his arm away. 'And I risked plenty breaking you from that cell, so if anyone owes anyone anything, it's you.'

Tanner waved his arms in a circle, signifying the encampment and the wagon.

'And *this* is how I'm repaying you. What we have ourselves here is a fine situation. A quarter share is worth getting when we've done most of the dangerous work. We just need a few people like you for one last deal.'

'I like the sound of that.' Dave patted his gunbelt. 'But I ain't much use with a gun, so what you're planning don't sit with my talents.'

Dave tipped his hat and turned.

'And what are your talents?' Waldo asked.

Dave rocked back and forth on his heels, then turned back.

'I sneak into places. I earn people's trust.' He glanced at Tanner. 'I get people out of places. I talk my way out of trouble.'

Waldo nodded. 'Tanner is right. Those are the sort of talents we're looking for. It'd be profitable for you to stay.'

Dave rubbed his chin and glanced up at the overhanging rocks and the surrounding boulders.

'I'll think on it. Maybe you'll see me later – if you're still around.'

Waldo shrugged, then ripped his gun from its holster and aimed it at Dave's head.

With a strangulated cry, Dave raised his hands and

backed a pace, but Waldo advanced two long strides and slammed the gun barrel against Dave's temple.

'Nobody leaves here. You're either with us, or you ain't.'

Dave gulped. 'If you put it like that, I'm with you.'

'But you didn't join willingly, so you got yourself some trouble. How are you going to talk me out of pulling the trigger?'

Dave rocked his gaze up to glance at the gun, then tore his gaze away to stare into Waldo's eyes.

'I don't rightly know how to stop you doing that,' he babbled, 'but there's one thing I know and that's that you don't want to kill me. You were all set to let me go. Then you pulled a gun on me when you didn't have to. Now, putting that together, I reckon that what's on your mind is a—'

'Quit babbling and give me a reason.'

'I was coming to that. Now the way I'm seeing it, you're out here miles from anywhere and you got some plans—'

'Give me a reason!' Waldo thrust the gun deeper into Dave's temple.

Dave strained his neck to cringe from the gun, but Waldo grabbed his chin and held him firm. The skin buckled and whitened around the barrel.

'I'm doing that. Your plans are forming, but you don't know how you'll get hold of certain info—'

'Enough!' Waldo pulled back from Dave and with a long round-armed slug from his left hand, knocked him on his back.

Dave slid four feet before coming to a halt. He lay a moment, then sat and stared up at Waldo, rubbing his chin. Waldo was pointing a firm finger at Dave's horse.

'I can go?' Dave asked.

'Yeah.' Waldo holstered his gun. 'You ain't worth killing and you were right the first time. You got no talent we need.'

Dave glanced at Waldo's holster. 'Talked you out of shooting me, didn't I?'

'You didn't. You just droned on and on until I got so annoyed with . . .' Waldo lowered his head a moment. When he looked up, his thin smile emerged. 'I suppose you did.'

Dave grinned. 'Then I'm with you – provided you want me talk my way out of trouble and not shoot my way.'

Waldo nodded. 'Seems a fair deal.'

Dave rolled to his feet and walked between Avery and Waldo to head for the fire, but Waldo grabbed his arm and pointed him towards the wagon.

'But that don't mean you're in. You've only earned the right to see Mendosa. He's in the wagon and as always, he ain't in a good mood.'

Dave glanced at Tanner, who provided an encouraging nod, then gulped and sauntered away from Waldo.

At the wagon, he stopped a moment to take a deep breath, then lifted the flap and levered himself inside.

A solitary man was inside sitting cross-legged. Around him, tottering stacks of crates left just enough space for him to sit and another man to sit opposite him.

Mendosa kept his gaze down, the brim of his hat hiding his face. With a short gesture, he signified that Dave should sit.

Dave sat, cross-legged, before Mendosa.

For long moments he stared at Mendosa's hat. Then, inch by inch Mendosa looked up.

A gleaming smile appeared first, then a broken nose, then the eyes. They were blue and lively and seemed capable of understanding a man within moments. The eyes narrowed.

'You're late,' Mendosa said, his tone calm. 'You should have been here a week ago.'

'I'm sorry.' Dave smiled. 'But I had me some organizing to do first.'

CHAPTER 10

After his discussion with Mendosa, Dave joined the men around the fire.

Waldo watched his every movement, but didn't talk to him about what had happened in the wagon. Dave presumed that his ability to survive his encounter with Mendosa provided all the details he needed.

With nothing else to do, he joined the game of chuck-a-luck, losing the last of his money with no reward other than providing amusement to his new colleagues. Then he shuffled from the game and huddled under a blanket.

He didn't talk to Tanner. But they'd had all the discussion they needed long ago and they'd agreed that appearing too friendly would raise suspicions that he had an ulterior motive in being here.

Long into the night, he whittled on a branch and piece by piece fed the scrapings to the fire, but while he worked, he was appraising his new associates. In his view, aside from Waldo, most were just the usual low-life dregs – heavy on arrogance and low on ambition.

When everyone else was asleep, Dave rolled over and slept too. Under his blanket, he spent a cold, restless night on the hard ground.

In the morning the men discussed the forthcoming deal while eating. Dave concentrated on his food, feigning no interest in their discussion, but he listened to every word, and they only went to confirm the details he'd discussed with Mendosa.

Throughout, Mendosa stayed in the wagon. Nobody viewed this as strange.

As soon as he dared, Dave shared low words with Tanner, then headed for his horse.

From behind he heard footfalls and from their weight he guessed that Waldo was following him, but he kept his gaze set forward.

'Where you going?' Waldo grunted.

Dave glanced over his shoulder, but didn't halt his journey towards his horse.

'Back to Stone Creek,' he said and mounted his horse. 'Mendosa said I could come and go as I pleased.'

'Why?'

'Because I want everyone to see that I'm still around.' Dave smiled and lifted the reins. 'Just in case I need to use my contacts later to talk us out of trouble.'

Waldo rubbed his chin as he considered. He nodded.

'I accept that. You can go.'

'I am going.' Dave tugged hard on the reins. 'But I don't need your permission.'

Waldo's eyes flared and he dashed towards him,

grunting his annoyance, but before he could restart the argument, Dave galloped from the encampment.

He took the most direct route out of Hard Gulch and headed back on to the trail to Stone Creek, only slowing when he'd confirmed that Waldo wasn't following him, then headed for the prearranged meeting-place on the edge of Snakepass Gully.

Rourke and Irwin were waiting for him.

'You kept us waiting,' Rourke muttered as he glowered at Dave.

Dave smiled. 'Brother, it ain't easy to leave Mendosa's gun-runners.'

'Quit complaining. You suggested doing this.'

Irwin edged his horse forward. 'Just tell us what you've got.'

Dave took a deep breath. 'Mendosa has at least fifty crates of rifles.'

'We know that,' Rourke snapped. 'That's why we want him.'

'Rourke,' Irwin murmured. 'Dave's confirmed that Mendosa still has the rifles, which we didn't know before.'

Rourke snorted, then forced a nod. 'Suppose we didn't. Go on.'

Dave edged his horse a pace closer. 'Mendosa was aiming to sell the rifles to a Sioux chief named Conchisto, but when he tried to contact him, he ran into some problems. But he's close to setting up a new deal.'

'That's good work,' Irwin said. He glanced at Rourke. 'Ain't that so?'

'If we can trust the messenger, it is,' Rourke

murmured, his face set in a deep sneer. 'So, how many are in Mendosa's gang?'

'Nine.'

'Where's he hiding?'

'Mendosa moves around. He'll be long gone from last night's camp.' Dave tapped his temple. 'But I've been thinking.'

'You ain't here to think,' Rourke grunted. 'Just tell us where last night's camp was.'

'I can, but I reckon that if you wait, you can round up Mendosa and his new contact in one go. You only have to wait a day or so and you'll stop all the gun-running in your territory.'

Rourke glared back, but Irwin nodded.

'Rourke,' Irwin said. 'He's speaking a lot of sense.'

'He ain't,' Rourke muttered.

'I am,' Dave said, sneering. 'And I reckon that if anyone else had suggested that, you'd have agreed to the change of plan, but just because it's me, you're rejecting it.'

'You're right. But that's because if anyone else had suggested it, I might have trusted them.'

'Put your feelings about Dave aside for just one moment,' Irwin said. 'And think this through.'

As Rourke glanced away, muttering to himself, Dave nodded.

'Your deputy's right. I got nothing to gain either way – I'm heading to Denver as soon as this is over – but you have a lot to gain.'

For long moments Rourke glared at Dave. Then, with a smack of his hand against his leg, he gave a curt nod.

76

'Go back to Mendosa. Find out where this deal is happening and meet us here at sundown.'

'But I can't ask questions. I have to wait until I hear something.'

'Sundown,' Rourke snapped, 'or we start doing this my way.'

With a short stab of his index finger, Rourke tipped his hat to Dave, then swung his horse around and galloped back down the trail.

Irwin waited a moment, staring at Dave.

Dave smiled. 'Thanks for speaking up for me.'

'I wasn't,' Irwin said. 'I'm just looking at the situation all impartial-like. And just like Rourke looks at everyone but you.' Irwin tipped his hat, then turned his horse. 'And I'm just hoping you don't make me regret it.'

As the two lawmen entered Stone Creek, Irwin rode alongside Rourke, considering Rourke's firm-jawed expression from the corner of his eye.

'I don't have to ask what you think of Dave's plan,' Irwin said.

'You guessed right,' Rourke muttered. 'And I don't have to ask what you think of it.' Rourke pulled up outside the sheriff's office and dismounted. He tethered his horse and stood on the boardwalk. 'But I do want to know why you're supporting him.'

'I ain't supporting him,' Irwin said, joining him. 'But the chance to capture Mendosa, and perhaps another gun-runner, and the chance to reclaim all those guns are things you used to support.'

For long moments Rourke hung his head, then

stalked down the boardwalk to the sheriff's office.

'I do still support those things.' Rourke kicked open the door but still held it open for Irwin. 'But I don't like letting Dave control us.'

Irwin wandered past Rourke and into the office.

'Neither do I, but Dave's taking a bigger risk than either of us.'

Rourke followed Irwin inside. 'And I can't clear that worry from my mind. That man can't erect a few fence-posts in return for a place to sleep without wheedling out of his responsibilities. So why is he risking his life just to earn my respect?'

'I don't reckon he'd cross the road to earn your respect.' Irwin shrugged. 'But perhaps he might risk his life to earn his own respect.'

Rourke snorted and headed for the stove.

'And that's the most unlikely explanation of all. He lost interest in respect years ago.'

'So you reckon he's double-crossing us?'

Rourke grabbed the coffee-pot from the stovetop and lifted the lid. He sniffed the contents, then turned to Irwin.

'Dave doesn't think that way. He survives from day to day. Whenever he sees an opportunity, he takes it. So he's just stringing this situation along, hoping that something will happen that he can turn to his advantage.'

'Perhaps he is, but I don't care if it removes that many gun-runners.'

'Yeah, but however I look at it, Dave is just enjoying himself too much.' Rourke slammed the pot back on the stove. 'And that never cheers me.'

*

'I told you to stay here,' Waldo muttered, glaring at Dave with his hands on his hips.

'Like I said,' Dave said as he dismounted his horse, 'Mendosa accepts me coming and going.'

Waldo glanced at the wagon. 'Mendosa might, but I don't. And until he leaves that wagon and tells me otherwise, I tell you what to do.'

'You're telling me nothing.' Dave glanced around the other men, but on receiving nothing but icy stares, he sighed then stalked towards Waldo to stand two paces before him. 'I come when I please and I go when I please. That's how I use my talents.'

Waldo glared back, then licked his lips and shrugged.

'You're right. You can get on your horse and leave camp whenever you want to.'

Dave tipped back his hat. 'Obliged.'

Waldo smirked and thrust his squat legs wide.

'Just don't expect to live long enough to ride out of camp.' Waldo unhooked his gunbelt and dropped it on top of his belongings then cracked his knuckles. 'And if you don't accept that, this is your only warning.'

Seeing no choice, Dave rolled his shoulders and squared off to Waldo with his fists raised.

'I ain't following your orders.'

Waldo met Dave's gaze, then glanced away. Without warning, he swung back and thundered a blow at Dave's jaw.

Dave rocked back from the blow, but it still clipped

his chin and wheeled him to the ground.

He lay a moment, exaggerating his hurt by wincing and shaking his head, then staggered to his feet.

Waldo swaggered towards him and in misplaced confidence swung a slow heavy blow at Dave's head, but Dave easily rocked back, then weighed in with a flurry of blows that pummelled Waldo to the ground.

As Waldo lay back, rubbing his chest, the remainder of the gun-runners dashed in to form a circle. They urged Waldo to get up and fight. Nobody cheered Dave on.

Dave stalked around the edge of the circle, keeping Waldo in his view as Waldo rolled to his feet. Then Waldo dashed at him with his head down, aiming to bundle him over.

Dave danced to the side and helped Waldo on his way with a flat-handed swipe to the back that hurled him through the circle of men and to the ground.

As Waldo extricated himself from the tangle of fallen bodies, Dave patted his hands together and strode round to face him.

'Pummel him,' Ty Jackson shouted.

'Grind his face into the dirt,' Eli Milton muttered.

Waldo stood tall with the encouragement and strode towards Dave.

As Dave backed from him, he glanced around the circle of men, smiling to himself, but his gaze picked out Tanner.

Tanner gave a short shake of his head.

Dave returned a nod, then turned to face the advancing Waldo.

Waldo stalked in, his jaw set firm, his eyes blazing,

and threw a long punch at Dave's jaw. The blow came far slower than before and Dave could have easily avoided it, but he only rolled back a foot, letting the blow smash into his jaw. He staggered in a short circle, bent double.

With a whoop of delight, Waldo leapt at him and slammed an arm around his shoulders, then smashed his fist up into Dave's guts.

Dave leapt from the ground with the blow, gasping, then folded over a second blow.

Waldo stood him straight and hurled a firm punch at his face.

Dave stood his ground and let the punch smash into his cheek. Still, it came harder than he expected and without exaggeration, he wheeled back and into the circle of men, but they threw him back to meet a pole-axing blow to the jaw.

Dave collapsed, the blow spinning him round to land flat on his belly. He pushed his arms down, but they shook and he lay flat.

'That's your only warning,' Waldo said, standing over him. 'Any more arguments from you and you won't get up, ever.'

On the ground, Dave rolled over on to his back and glared up at Waldo, but then lowered his gaze and gave a short nod.

Waldo spat on Dave's boots, then swaggered past him, grinding his heel into the dirt inches from Dave's right hand before disappearing into a huddle of backslapping.

Only Tanner went to Dave's side and helped him sit up.

'Losing that fight was the right thing to do,' Tanner whispered.

'Perhaps.' Dave glanced at Waldo's back. 'But I still need to see Rourke at sundown.'

'Quit worrying about him. You've distracted the lawmen enough.'

'I covered my tracks, but they might be able to work out where we are and then . . .'

Tanner blew out his cheeks, but then nodded.

'Sundown.' Tanner glanced at Waldo. 'And then I reckon we just have to sort him out.'

CHAPTER 11

Throughout a long day, Dave stalked around the encampment, but although he didn't come within fifty yards of his horse, Waldo's gaze never left him.

Dave didn't return the gaze, ensuring he maintained his downtrodden act. But he did talk with everyone whom he wandered past.

He avoided mentioning the gun-runners' plans and, although he didn't find any potential allies he could use to take on Waldo, from everyone he detected an acceptance that he was the kind of person who was a bad fighter but was otherwise reliable.

An hour before sundown, Waldo took Mendosa's meal into his wagon, then returned to sit by the fire, but his gaze bored into Dave.

For the first time Dave returned his gaze, then lowered his head, but as he shovelled his meal into his mouth, Waldo swaggered to his feet and sauntered around the fire until he loomed over Dave.

'You ignoring me?' he muttered.

'Nope,' Dave said. 'I'm just eating.'

Waldo nodded, then with a round-footed kick, knocked the plate from Dave's grasp. The plate landed face down, flattening the food into the dirt.

'Now you ain't eating. You can't ignore me.'

Dave looked up to meet Waldo's gaze a moment, then rolled on to his haunches and prised the plate over. Piece by piece he shovelled the stew back on to his plate, then sat and resumed eating, swallowing hard to gulp down the grit.

Waldo's shadow stayed over him. Then Waldo snorted and made a gesture that Dave didn't see, but which dragged a laugh from Ty and Eli, then everyone else around the fire.

Dave just shovelled the grit-filled food into his mouth and swallowed, and eventually Waldo snorted and swaggered back to his place by the fire. Dave glanced up at his receding back, then shared a glance and a short smile with Tanner.

With Dave refusing to let Waldo goad him into another fight, Waldo lost all interest in him and within minutes of sundown, he'd retired to sleep beside the fire. Within a half-hour, all the other men retired to sleep except for Tanner, who had volunteered to take the first watch.

Dave waited until he heard snoring from all the men, then rolled from his blanket. For twenty paces he edged backwards from the fire, but as he didn't detect any change in the rhythm of the snoring, he turned and headed to his horse.

Tanner tipped his hat to him.

'I won't be on guard when you get back,' he whispered.

Dave shrugged. 'Suppose I'll worry about that problem later.'

Tanner nodded and gestured for him to leave.

Dave grabbed his horse's reins and walked it away from the encampment, but then slowed to a halt and turned. He gestured for Tanner to join him out of hearing-range of the men around the fire.

'What's wrong?' Tanner asked.

Dave sighed. 'Are you still fine with what we're doing here?'

Tanner narrowed his eyes. 'You ain't having second thoughts, are you?'

'Kind of. I've always avoided trouble – except when I'm drunk – but I couldn't avoid that fight with Waldo and it made me realize just how much danger we're facing here. If you hadn't persuaded me to let Waldo win, he'd probably have gone for his gun and killed me.'

For long moments Tanner stared at Dave, but then sighed and patted his shoulder.

'To be honest the likes of Waldo don't worry me, but those crates of rifles do. Even if we get away with this, they could still end up in the wrong hands.'

Dave nodded. 'So you reckon we should just walk away from this?'

Tanner glanced at the fire, then at the wagon.

'We can't walk away. We're in deep with Mendosa, and I don't reckon he takes kindly to anyone who crosses him.'

'So what you're saying is we're in a whole mess of trouble if we go through with this and a whole mess of trouble if we don't.'

'Yup. And at least by going through with this we're in a whole mess of trouble and rich.'

Dave sighed and mounted his horse.

'Or maybe just dead and rich.'

Dave turned his horse and paced down into the gulch. But then, when he was 200 yards down the gulch, he shrugged and speeded to a gallop.

Within ten minutes he emerged on to the plains and, as the arc of light thinned on the western horizon, he reached the meeting-point.

Rourke and Irwin were waiting for him.

'You're late,' Rourke muttered. 'Again.'

'I'm doing my best.' Dave smiled as he raised his hands. 'And don't I get some praise for all the good work I'm doing? I'm risking my life here.'

'You'll get some praise when I've captured Mendosa and his gun-runners,' Rourke muttered. 'But until you've earned my respect, you're just another unreliable source of information.'

Irwin shuffled his horse forward three paces to stand between Rourke and Dave.

'Just back down, you two,' he said. 'I want to know what Dave's discovered.'

Dave glared at Rourke over Irwin's shoulder a moment, then nodded.

'In return for gold Mendosa is selling his rifles to someone called Miguel Duttoni.'

'The worst gun-runner around,' Irwin murmured. He glanced back at Rourke, who nodded.

'Yeah,' Rourke said. 'Information like that is starting to earn my respect. What else you got?'

'The deal is tomorrow afternoon.'

'Where?'

'I don't know.'

Rourke slammed a fist against his thigh.

'You ugly varmint. Tell me.'

'I ain't holding out on you. I just don't know.'

'You expect me to believe that you've found out who Mendosa is selling his rifles to and when he's doing it, but not where?'

'Yeah. I ain't been asking questions. I just listen to everyone talk and that information just ain't been said. But I reckon nobody knows. Mendosa has done the deal with Duttoni and he never leaves the wagon where he's stored the rifles.'

'You reckon you can find out where it's happening before the deal?' Irwin asked.

'I reckon so.'

'Obliged.'

Rourke and Irwin shared a long look.

'Stone Creek tomorrow morning,' Rourke muttered. Then he shook his head and turned his horse. With his head down, he rode away.

'No need to thank me, brother,' Dave shouted after him.

Rourke pulled his horse to a halt and waited a moment, then rode on.

Dave tipped his hat to Irwin, receiving a harsh warning glare in return. Then Irwin turned and hurried on to join Rourke.

Dave watched their backs recede into the gloom, then turned his horse and headed back towards Mendosa's encampment.

For a hundred yards or so he rode at a walking

pace. Then, with a shrug, he dismissed his troubles from his mind and hurried his horse to a trot.

'Put those hands high,' a voice muttered.

Dave darted his gaze in all directions, but the crescent moon only provided enough light to see the trail ahead, the trees surrounding him, and the crags etched against the night sky. He pulled hard on the reins, ready to gallop away, but then twenty yards ahead, a man strode out from behind a tree, a rifle to his shoulder and aimed at Dave's head.

Lacking any obvious choice, Dave pulled his horse to a halt and lifted his hands from the reins.

From the trees surrounding him, more men paced into view and with his eyes narrowed Dave recognized the forms of Waldo, Ty and Eli. Each of these men had his gun pulled and levelled on him.

With his rifle, Waldo gestured for Dave to dismount.

Keeping his movements steady, Dave dismounted and stalked towards Waldo, keeping his hands at chest-level with the palms facing down. He swung to a halt.

'What you want?' he asked.

Waldo stalked sideways to stand three paces before Dave.

'Why were you meeting those two lawmen from Stone Creek?'

'I can tell you,' Dave said. 'But it's a mighty long story.'

'Then cut it short.' Waldo glanced at Ty and Eli, who both firmed their gun hands, then swung the rifle round to hold it sideways to Dave. 'But if you try that babbling trick again, I'll just shoot you.'

'Then I'll try to—'

Waldo advanced two long paces and swung the rifle round to slam the butt deep into Dave's guts.

Dave folded over the blow and staggered to the side only to receive a side-handed chop on the back of his neck that knocked him to the ground. Hands bundled him over and ripped his gun from its holster, then pulled him to his feet.

Dave shook his head to clear his vision, but by then Ty and Eli were dragging him to the side. With rough hands they slammed him back against a tree and pinned him there. He looked up to see that he was facing Waldo, who with a firm gesture swung his rifle up and aimed it straight between Dave's eyes. He grinned, his teeth a slash of white in the darkness.

'You got ten seconds to be mighty convincing.'

'Do you want to hear what I got to say?' Dave murmured. 'Or are you just looking to kill me?'

'I am looking to kill you, but if you tell me a mighty fine tale, I might not. Now talk!' He spat to the side. 'One.'

Dave rolled his shoulders and stood tall.

'I was just talking to Sheriff Bowman and Deputy Francis.'

'I saw that. Tell me something I don't know.' Waldo edged his rifle up a mite to sight Dave's forehead. 'Two.'

'Sheriff Bowman is my brother,' Dave shouted.

Waldo's rifle barrel wavered a moment, before he controlled his surprise with a shake of his head.

'If that's a lie, it's a stupid one. Three.'

'It ain't a lie. I had my reasons and they ain't about double-crossing you. I'm just bargaining with him to get information on the times and locations of the next arms shipment to Fort Stirling.'

'We have our sources and at the moment we're only interested in dealing with Miguel Duttoni. Four.'

'I know, but like I said, I have talents. I have contacts. I talk to people. I get information. And I ain't much use sitting around at the camp.'

Waldo nodded. 'Five. I can see that. So, your story is that you're with us and you're double-crossing your own brother.'

'That pretty much sums it up.'

'And your story ain't that you're working with your brother to double-cross us?' Waldo rolled his shoulders. 'Six.'

'Guess you might find it hard to believe and if I were in your place I wouldn't believe it either, but I ain't working with him.'

Waldo firmed his arm. 'Seven. I don't know you well enough to trust you.'

'Perhaps, but before you shoot me, check with Mendosa.'

'Why?'

'Because he knows that I'm Sheriff Bowman's brother. It won't concern him that I met him.'

Waldo lowered the rifle and glanced at Ty and Eli in turn. Both men muttered their disbelief.

'Mendosa wouldn't keep that from us,' Waldo snapped. He raised his rifle. 'Eight.'

'He had to. He knew how you'd react.'

'He's right. We can't have you talking to lawmen.' Waldo licked his lips, his eyes bright. 'Nine.'

'And how do you think you get information for planning raids?' Dave shouted. 'You have to meet people and talk. And that's what I do.'

Waldo's trigger finger wavered. Then he relaxed it and glanced at Ty.

'What you reckon, Ty?'

'His ten seconds are up,' Ty muttered. 'Shoot him.'

Waldo nodded. 'And you, Eli?'

'Don't shoot him,' Eli said. He chuckled and mimed a noose tightening. 'String him up and stretch his neck instead.'

Waldo widened his eyes and glared at Dave.

'Seems like we don't believe your story. Te—'

'Wait!' Dave shouted. 'Just check with Mendosa first.'

'We don't need to take orders on everything from Mendosa.'

'You don't. But if you kill me, Mendosa's plans will fail and he will kill you.' Dave smiled. 'But if I'm lying, you'll still get the chance to kill me.'

Waldo's eyes blazed, but inch by inch he lowered his gun.

'Perhaps I should check,' he murmured.

'You won't regret it.'

Waldo snorted, then gestured for Eli and Ty to release him.

'I won't, because when I've checked, I will be killing you – either tonight or tomorrow.'

CHAPTER 12

'Mendosa,' Waldo roared as he rode back into the encampment. 'Get out here, now!'

Eli dragged Dave from his horse and pushed him forward a pace so that he faced the wagon.

Dave stood tall, but Waldo slammed his rifle butt down on Dave's right shoulder, forcing him to his knees. On the ground his gaze sought out Tanner, who sat by the fire, but his friend gulped and glanced away, shaking his head.

All eyes turned to the wagon as Mendosa lifted the cloth and peered out, then jumped to the ground. With a slow slip of a finger, he tipped back his hat and glared down at Dave on the ground. His eyes narrowed a moment. Then he faced Waldo.

'You called me from the wagon,' he murmured.

Waldo pointed at Dave. 'Yeah, but Dave was double-crossing us.'

'And?'

'And his brother is Sheriff Bowman and he was meeting him.'

Mendosa shrugged. 'I didn't ask what he was doing. I want to know why you're wasting my time telling me this.'

'Dave stopped me killing him by saying that you knew his brother was a lawman, so before I killed him, I brought him here so I could hear whether that was true.'

Mendosa walked two paces to look down at Dave. They shared a glance. Then he shrugged and turned away. He glanced at Tanner as he sauntered back to his wagon, but with a hand on the wagon side, he stopped.

'That's a lie,' he murmured.

'Hey,' Dave shouted. 'You got to tell him that—'

Waldo slammed his rifle butt on the back of Dave's head, flattening him, then paced forward to stand over him.

'And what should I do with him?' he asked.

'That's your concern.' Mendosa lifted a foot to the wagon. 'But if you want to live, don't call for me again.'

As Mendosa swung into the wagon, Dave shuffled round on the ground to look up at Waldo.

'Don't,' he murmured.

'I sure am,' Waldo muttered and swung his rifle round to aim it down at Dave.

'You ain't!' Tanner shouted, striding from the fire.

'Keep out of this,' Waldo snapped. 'Dave is a double-crosser.'

'That's as maybe, but he broke me out of a cell.' Tanner ripped his gun from its holster and aimed it at Waldo. 'And you ain't killing him.'

From the corner of his eye Waldo glanced at Tanner and snorted.

'If you side with this varmint, I'll kill you just as soon as I've killed Dave.'

Tanner shook his head. 'You ain't. The only thing you're doing is stepping away from Dave.'

Waldo glanced around the arc of men beside him.

'You can't count, Tanner. There are more of us than you got bullets in that gun. You ain't ordering anyone.'

To Waldo's taunt, every other man in the site shuffled round to face Tanner and turned their guns on him.

'The only person I'm ordering is you. Before anyone shoots me, I'll have ended your sorry existence.'

Waldo glared at Tanner, then snorted and backed a pace from Dave.

'You're siding with the wrong man, Tanner. Dave was selling us out to those lawmen.'

'I only got your story to back that up and I don't trust you.' Tanner firmed his gun hand. 'But I do trust a man that breaks me out of a cell, and I reckon I'll give Dave a chance to explain himself.'

'Pity you won't live for long after you've heard him.'

Waldo glanced around the arc of men holding guns on Tanner, but then nodded and one by one they lowered their guns.

Dave rolled to his feet and sidled away from Waldo to join Tanner. Walking backwards, they edged to their horses. With Tanner keeping his gun on Waldo,

Dave mounted his horse first. Then he and Tanner rolled into their saddles and, in a flurry of dust, galloped from the encampment.

As they cleared the overhanging rock, Waldo dashed for his horse, but Tanner fired over his shoulder. The lead winged ten feet over Waldo's head, but it still forced him to slide to a halt and lift his hands.

At a gallop they rounded the sentinel rocks at the edge of the encampment, and just as the camp disappeared from view, Dave glanced back to see Waldo and at least three others dashing for their horses. Behind them, the wagon was as closed as it ever was.

They hurtled down the gulch, heading for the open plains.

For three minutes they pushed their horses to their limit as they gained as much distance between themselves and Waldo as they could, but just as their steeds began to strain and sweat, they pulled hard to the right and hurtled into cover between two large rocks.

They had no time to return and cover their tracks, having to trust instead the hardness of the ground, the speed of the following men, and the weak moonlight.

They leapt down from their horses, pulled their guns, and pressed back against the rocks on either side of the gap to disappear into the shadows.

Less than a minute later, Waldo and a string of riders hurtled past them. When they'd galloped past, Dave edged out to count them, finding that only two men had stayed back at the encampment.

For another minute they waited for the riders to

disappear around the next bend in the gulch, then leapt on their horses and hurtled back in the other direction.

As they passed the encampment, they kept their heads low and galloped hard, but if anyone was guarding the encampment and saw them, they didn't pursue.

As they rounded every corner in the twisting gulch, both men glanced back, but still no pursuit was coming, so by the time the gulch opened at the other side, both men slowed.

'You should have stopped Waldo from following me,' Dave shouted.

'I ain't taking that.' Tanner shook a fist at Dave. 'This is your fault. You should have been more careful. We took months to set this up. Then you ruin everything with one stupid act.'

'Perhaps.' Dave sneered. 'But whoever's fault it is, Mendosa should have supported me.'

Tanner glanced over his shoulder, but he saw only the deserted gulch receding behind him.

'What did you expect him to say? That he knew you were Rourke's brother, but he didn't say anything?'

Dave also glanced back, then nodded.

'It'd have helped.'

'He had no choice. Before he'd explained that, Waldo and just about everyone else would have filled him with bullets.'

Dave sighed. 'Well, at least that means our deals with him are off. We can walk away from this now.'

'I don't reckon so. Mendosa nodded to me. I took

that to mean that I should save you. So I reckon our plans are still in place.'

Dave winced. 'A pity. So, what are those plans now?'

'To be honest,' Tanner murmured, tipping back his hat, 'I got no idea.'

CHAPTER 13

With his gun drawn, Rourke edged into the doorway to his barn.

The two men he'd just seen scurrying inside were lurking in the shadows. A third man was huddled with them.

Rourke glanced at each man in turn, at least confirming that two of them were Dave and Barton.

'Who's that with you, Dave?' he shouted.

Dave grinned, his smile bright in the gloom.

'This is Tanner Eldridge, brother,' he shouted.

Rourke took a long pace into the barn and aimed his gun at Tanner.

'Then put your hands up, Tanner.' With his gun held before him, Rourke paced three paces into the barn. 'I'm arresting you for gun-running.'

Rourke pointed at Tanner's gunbelt and gestured for him to remove it.

With a glance at Dave, Tanner followed his orders, then lifted his hands high.

'I can explain myself, Sheriff,' he said. 'I was with Mendosa, but Dave and me got talking. He's heading to Denver to set up a business and he's offered to cut me in. That sounds far better than gun-running to me.'

Rourke snorted a harsh chuckle.

'You're right, but no matter what Dave's promised you, I can't ignore your former crimes.'

Tanner edged a pace closer to Rourke and smiled.

'Even if I help you bring in Quinn Mendosa and Miguel Duttoni?'

'Nope. Now head to your horse. I'm taking you into town.' Rourke gestured with his gun towards the door, then shrugged. 'But I will ensure that Judge Daniels in Beaver Ridge takes into consideration the fact that you turned yourself in. If that impresses him, you'll get that chance to join Dave in his *business* before too long.'

Tanner strode forward another pace and stamped a foot.

'I didn't come here to end up in no jail. I came here to help you.'

'You don't want to help me.' Rourke advanced across the barn and slammed a firm hand on Tanner's shoulder, then pushed him towards the barn door. 'The only person you want to help is yourself.'

'You're right.' Tanner skidded to a halt and turned. 'And I reckon a share in the reward money for capturing Mendosa will help me plenty.'

Rourke scuffed the dirt at his feet as he shook his head.

'And there it is. I *do* believe that.' Rourke glanced at Dave and sneered. 'But it just calls you into question. That talk of helping me track down Mendosa to make me proud of you was rot. You just saw a Wanted poster in my office and realized how much money you could make from this.'

Dave glanced away, then shrugged.

'Ain't lying to you,' he said. 'I did do that. I reckoned that one thousand dollars was a fair price when I only had to find Mendosa.'

Rourke nodded. 'All right. Now I've heard some truth, tell me the rest. Where can I find him?'

Dave and Tanner shared a glance. Then Dave stepped forward.

'Mendosa's dealing with Duttoni tomorrow afternoon at Diamond Ridge.'

'That's good information, and if it's accurate, it'll get you that reward money.' Rourke glanced at Tanner. 'And keep you out of jail.'

'Obliged,' Tanner said.

'But that ain't all we got,' Dave said. 'If Duttoni sees any weakness in Mendosa, he'll try to keep his gold, but come away with the guns.'

'But Mendosa ain't worried,' Tanner said. 'I was part of his back-up. Until I saved Dave, three other men and me were to lie in wait at the ridge. When Mendosa gave the signal, we were to open fire and double-cross Duttoni before he could double-cross us.'

'But now, with our help you can get Mendosa, Duttoni, and the other gun-runners.' Dave raised his voice as Rourke grunted his lack of interest. 'We ambush the back-up on the way to Diamond Ridge, then let Mendosa and Duttoni get into a gunfight.

100

We let that play out, then arrest whoever survives.'

'There ain't no *we*,' Rourke snapped. 'And I ain't letting a gun battle rage when I can stop it.'

'You ain't got the firepower to do anything else. You just got two lawmen and us two.'

'And me,' Barton said, jumping to his feet. 'I want in on this too. I could do plenty with a share of that reward.'

'Yeah,' Dave said. 'You could pay for that window you broke in the Golden Star.'

'You broke it,' Barton whined.

Rourke snorted as he appraised Barton. 'Either way, I suppose two lawmen and two and a half back-ups might be enough. But as I ain't interested, we'll never find out.'

'Just think about our plan, brother,' Dave said. 'Sometimes thinking can get a better result than charging in with your gun blazing.'

Rourke rubbed his chin, then shrugged.

'I'll think about it.'

'And if you reckon it's a good idea,' Barton said with a sly grin, 'does that mean I get deputized?'

Rourke winced and stalked from the barn. As he headed to his house, the first twinge of a headache tapped at his temples.

Harlan leapt into bed, drew the covers to his chin and rasped a snore. With his eyes clamped shut, he heard the door open and his mother pace inside, but he snored again, and she backed and closed the door.

Harlan cracked open an eye, confirmed that the

room was empty, then slipped from the bed and listened at the door. Within a minute, his parents returned to their muttered argument.

He couldn't tell what they arguing about but the repeated mentioning of Dave told him that his uncle must have returned this evening. When he heard his father mention the barn for the second time, he nodded to himself. But with this confirmation, one of the many worries that had assailed him since Dave had left plagued his thoughts.

Ten minutes of brooding later, he dressed quietly, then padded to the window and slipped outside.

He edged around the outside of the house, then scurried to the barn using a wide arc to avoid anyone seeing him from the window. He shuffled around the side of the barn, then dashed through the doorway.

Propped up against the back wall were three men huddled under blankets. One of the men was Barton May. He didn't recognize the other man, but the third man was Dave.

Dave had an arm outside the blanket and was whittling on a branch, but on seeing Harlan, he pocketed the knife. Smiling, he shuffled to a sitting position and beckoned Harlan to approach.

'Howdy, nephew,' he said.

'Howdy, uncle.' Harlan shuffled across the barn to stand before Dave. He folded his hands across his belt, but as he couldn't meet Dave's gaze, hung his head. 'If they catch me here, I'll be in big trouble, but I didn't tell Pa about you saying that I should get Otto to hit Torn – honest I didn't.'

'What?'

Harlan edged another pace closer to Dave.

'Pa must have sent you away for a reason. But it wasn't my fault.'

Dave tipped back his hat to rub his forehead, then shrugged.

'Suppose I know that, nephew.'

Harlan grinned and backed a pace. 'Obliged. I didn't want you thinking that I told on you.'

Harlan turned and scampered to the door, but then slowed to halt. He glanced through the doorway at the house, seeing nobody at the window. While rocking his head from side to side, he patted a fist against his leg, then turned back.

'You sure there ain't anything else you want to say to me?' Dave said.

Despite the night chill, Harlan's cheeks warmed and sweat broke out on his brow, but he comforted himself with the thought that in the poor light, Dave probably wouldn't be able to see this. He edged back across the barn.

'There was . . .' Harlan screeched. He coughed to clear his throat and resumed in a calmer voice. 'There was one other thing I wanted to ask you, if you're not angry with me.'

Dave leaned back against the wall. 'Ask. That's what uncles are for.'

Harlan took a deep breath. 'I want some advice about how to talk to women . . . I mean girls . . . I mean . . .'

As Harlan hung his head, under their blankets the other two men chuckled. Dave joined in the laughter.

'I can tell you what I know.' Dave snorted. 'It won't take long.'

Harlan looked up. 'Anything you can tell me would help.'

Dave considered Harlan a moment, then leaned forward.

'Do you want advice about all women, or just one woman in particular?'

'Just the one – for now.'

Dave patted the ground beside the blanket.

'Then settle down. I have some ideas.'

Deep into the night, Rourke rode to Deputy Francis's house.

Standing outside on the darkened plains staring at the panoply of stars, he outlined the tale Tanner and Dave had told him, and all through his telling, Irwin continually kicked stones and shook his head.

'I guess from your dour tone,' Irwin said when Rourke had finished, 'that you don't believe a single word either man told you.'

'I don't know Tanner, but I know the type, and that goes for Dave too. But I trust your opinion. You're more objective than I am about Dave. What do you reckon?'

Irwin sighed and set his hands on his hips.

'You reckoned Dave had an ulterior motive all along, and it's possible that the reward is what he wanted.'

'Maybe, and if Tanner hadn't mentioned the reward, I might have realized that that was all Dave wanted, but Dave is a sneaky varmint. If that's what he's admitted he wants, he's probably after something else.'

'He could be, but I keep coming back to the same thought. I don't care what Dave's really after if it helps us get Mendosa and now Duttoni.'

'Suppose you're right.' Rourke turned to face Irwin's house. 'But even if they help, I ain't deputizing them. That would just be plain wrong. I have to trust my deputies.'

Irwin smiled. 'Glad to hear it. But what about Barton? Are you letting him come along?'

'I'll think about it,' Rourke muttered. He headed for his horse. With his face set in a sneer, he mounted it and raised the reins. 'But with Barton reckoning that it's a good enough idea to come along, I reckon it just proves how bad an idea it is.'

'Perhaps, but I reckon the real problem is that you just don't like being led by your brother.'

For long moments Rourke stared down at Irwin, then nodded.

'You're right. We need to seize control of this situation.' Rourke leaned down and grinned. 'So, are you ready for a night's hard riding?'

CHAPTER 14

For a moment Celeste's surprise froze her throat and she just opened and closed her mouth soundlessly.

For the last month, she'd sewn clothes for old Miss Fenshaw and she'd promised to bring a mended shawl into the store so that she could collect it this morning. But what with all the turbulence of Rourke ensuring that the men in the barn had left, and another argument with Rourke about Dave, she'd forgotten the shawl and had had to return to fetch it.

Like Rourke, she'd thought that Dave and the others might run long before they raided either group of gun-runners and that they'd return to lurk in the barn, so she'd glanced through the door to check that the barn was empty.

Neither Dave nor the other men were in the barn. But Harlan was.

And he wasn't alone.

'Get to school, *now*,' Celeste screamed when at last she regained her voice.

A red-faced Harlan and an equally red-faced

Millicent Lester flinched, separated, then scurried past her.

Harlan skidded to a halt and stood before Millicent. Tentatively he brushed her hand, but Millicent shrugged away from him and held her hands behind her back.

'We weren't doing anything,' he whimpered.

'Only because I came back.' She glanced at Millicent, who was edging from side to side. 'And you'll come with me, young lady. I'll ensure you both get to school – as you should have done an hour ago.'

Although Celeste was more surprised than annoyed, she maintained an appropriate level of punishing silence throughout her deliberately slow journey to school. And when Harlan and Millicent alighted from the cart at the school, she let a disapproving glare leave both of them in no doubt that the matter wasn't closed.

Although Rourke was facing a lot of trouble today, she decided that the incident might distract him from his brooding. So before starting work at Cartwright's store, she slipped into the sheriff's office.

Irwin and Rourke were huddled in debate, but when she entered Rourke directed Irwin to busy himself at the back of the office and turned to her.

In a few brief sentences she relayed the details of the incident in the barn.

Throughout, Rourke's eyes remained flared, but he clenched his jaw harder and harder until the muscles seemed set to burst.

'What do you reckon?' she asked when she'd finished her tale.

Rourke tipped his hat back on his head and slammed his hands on his hips.

'However I look at this, I can't believe Harlan got it into his head to take Josh Lester's daughter into our barn.'

Celeste shrugged. 'Two people decided to go into that barn.'

'And one of them was Harlan. He should be more responsible. He ain't old enough to be in no barn with no girl.'

'Perhaps you're right, but what they were doing was pretty innocent.' Celeste smiled and fluttered her eyelashes at Rourke. 'Besides, what were you doing when you were his age?'

'I wasn't in no barn.' Rourke folded his arms. 'And I guess neither were you.'

Celeste stood back and held her chin aloft.

'Then you guessed wrong. I was sure getting into barns when I was Millicent's age.'

'Celeste!'

'Quit whining. If I was as slow in coming forward as you are, we'd have never got together.'

'That was different. We're talking about Harlan and he was just plain wrong. And I want to know who put him up to it.'

'Somebody else isn't to blame every time Harlan does something you don't like. Sometimes it's all Harlan's idea.'

'Perhaps.' Rourke stalked to the window and stared outside. 'But Harlan didn't get ideas until Dave arrived.'

*

The lawmen collected Dave, Tanner and Barton from the Lucky Dip where they were gulping down a confidence-boosting last drink.

After Rourke issued a final round of instructions, they separated. Irwin and Tanner rode to Diamond Ridge. Dave, Barton and Rourke headed to Snakepass Gully.

For the first four miles of steady riding, Rourke maintained a brooding silence, but when his mixture of bemusement and anger had subsided to a grumbling ache in the guts, he beckoned Dave to ride alongside.

'Have you talked to Harlan since you returned to my barn?' he asked, his voice calm.

Dave kept his gaze forward. 'You told me not to talk to him no more, brother. What makes you think I have?'

'Because you don't do what I ask. And because Celeste returned home early and found that Harlan hadn't gone to school today.'

Dave turned in the saddle to face Rourke.

'I wouldn't encourage him to miss schooling.'

'Maybe not. But he was. And worse, he was in the barn with a girl.'

Dave's eyes widened and he glanced away, licking his lips to suppress a smile.

'He's mighty young for doing that. But it sounds to me like he'll grow into a fine man.'

'I ain't seeing anything funny about this. Before you arrived Harlan fought his own battles and had no interest in taking girls into barns.'

Dave lifted a hand from the reins a moment to hold it wide.

'You can't blame me for Harlan growing up.'

'I can if you're leading him in the wrong direction.'

'I'm his uncle,' Dave said, lowering his voice. 'Whatever you think of me, I promise you, I'd do nothing to hurt him.'

Rourke sighed and provided a begrudging nod.

'Suppose I know that, but that don't stop you causing mischief indirectly.'

Dave shrugged. 'If Harlan wants advice from his uncle, am I just supposed to say, see your pa?'

'Yeah.'

'Even if he wants to ask me about things he can't ask his pa?'

'Especially then.'

Dave turned in the saddle. For long moments he contemplated Rourke, then shook his head.

'What Harlan did this morning was something he was going to do one day whether he spoke to me or not, so you can't be mad at me just because of that. I've done nothing particularly bad in my life, yet you treat me as if I'm in league with Mendosa himself. So what's this really about?'

'This is just about Harlan and what you encouraged him to do this morning.'

'You mean you're annoyed because Harlan ain't as backward at talking to girls as you were at his age?'

'You wouldn't know,' Rourke snapped. 'You left home.'

Rourke pulled his horse to a halt. Barton glanced back at them, but Rourke beckoned him to ride ahead.

Dave halted his horse and hunched forward in the saddle.

'So that's what you're so irked about, brother. But I had to go. I wanted to see the world.'

'You didn't. Seeing the world was my dream. You were the older brother. You had to look after the farm.'

Dave glanced away a moment, nodding.

'And you got left with a farm you didn't have the courage to run away from.'

'It took more courage to stay. Pa put his whole life into building a life out here for his family. Except when we grew up, neither of us wanted that life. But you ran away first and made your own life.'

'I suppose I did, but you can't blame me for that.'

'I can, because what did you do with it?' Rourke hurled his hands in the air. 'You just frittered it away.'

Dave chuckled. 'To be honest, I kind of enjoyed myself.'

'Yeah. And that's because you ran away from your responsibilities. You let other people deal with them. And that's just what you're doing again. You'll enjoy yourself for a few days. Then you'll leave. But I'll have to live with what you've done for years.'

'They're mighty harsh words to describe a friendly bit of advice to my only nephew.'

'They ain't. If Celeste hadn't come home, maybe one day soon Harlan would have had to live with the result of *your* lack of responsibility for the rest of his life.'

'We all make our own choices in life.' Dave yanked on the reins and hurried on ahead. 'Then we live with them.'

CHAPTER 15

'Three men are coming,' Barton said, peering over the rock before him.

Rourke leaned to his side and pressed Barton's head below the rock.

'Then keep your head down,' he muttered, 'or you'll be facing a long drop when one of them shoots you.'

'Understood, boss.' Barton shuffled round and grinned up at Rourke. 'As I'm out here facing a dangerous gang of outlaws, I reckon I can ask you again – are you going to deputize me?'

Rourke snorted. 'No, but if you're really lucky I might trust you to finish my fence. Now, stay down.'

Rourke glared at Barton until he hunched down well below the top of the rock, then peered around the side of his covering boulder into Snakepass Gully. He confirmed that three riders were heading down the pass. One of them was the man who'd escaped when they'd captured Tanner.

'I recognize Avery,' Rourke said. 'Who are the others?'

'Don't know,' Barton whispered.

'I wasn't asking you.' Rourke glanced at Dave.

Dave edged to Rourke's side. 'Ty and Vernon – Mendosa's back-up.'

Rourke nodded and shuffled into a comfortable stance. He mouthed instructions to Dave and Barton, and the two men shuffled away with their heads low to take positions thirty yards away on either side of him.

When the riders were level with him below, he glanced at Barton, then at Dave. With his palms facing down, he ordered them to stay low. Then he swung out to perch a raised foot on the top of the boulder before him.

'Give yourself up!' he roared.

The men below flinched and glanced around before their gazes rose and centred on Rourke. As one they ripped out their guns and blasted lead at him. From such a distance all of it was wild.

Still, Rourke ducked. He smiled on seeing that Dave and Barton had taken his advice and had stayed down too.

When the first volley ended, Rourke glanced over the boulder.

The men had abandoned their horses and had taken cover. For a moment this surprised Rourke, as he'd planned for a long chase and had stayed high in the gully so he could get to his horse quickly.

He shrugged away his surprise and gestured to Dave and Barton, but before he finished his instructions, another volley of gunfire blasted from below and gouged into the rocks around Barton. From the sharpness of the retort, Rourke reckoned it came from a closer position than the gully bottom.

'What you reckon?' Rourke shouted to Dave.

'We have the better position and they'll have to outflank us to stand a chance.'

Rourke nodded and ordered Barton and Dave to return fire, then slammed his gun on the top of the boulder and blasted shot after shot down the gully, only pausing to reload and blast again.

This sustained fire cannoned around the men's positions, and from such a distance they could probably avoid it all day, but it had the unexpected advantage of spooking their horses.

With a toss of their manes and their heels kicking up great gouts of dust, they scampered down the gully, but as they passed Vernon's and Ty's positions, the two men dashed out and lunged for their trailing reins.

Rourke hated shooting at fleeing men, but he gritted his teeth and blasted at them. On the third shot, he winged Vernon's shoulder, wheeling him to the ground. As he reloaded, a shot from Barton ripped into Vernon's back, knocking him flat.

As Rourke tipped his hat to Barton, Ty dashed for cover but another shot from Barton blasted into his chest. Ty staggered two paces, but his legs folded and he fell to his knees, then keeled over on to his front.

With unexpected respect forcing a smile from Rourke, he turned to Barton and beckoned him to take a position closer to him.

'Got to hand it to you, Barton.' he said. 'I didn't think you could shoot like that.'

'You didn't think I could build your fence, but I did.' Barton blew over the top of his gun barrel. 'I got me some hidden talents.'

Rourke glanced over his shoulder and beckoned Dave to come closer. Dave was shaking his head with the same level of bemusement that Rourke was feeling.

'So,' Rourke said, 'man with hidden talents, did you see Avery?'

'Nope, I—' Barton screeched and pointed over Rourke's right shoulder at the rock behind him – Avery was emerging to perch on top of it. 'There he is!'

As Barton swung on the hip, Avery leapt from the rock. Before Barton could fire he bundled Rourke to the ground, knocking his gun away. The two men rolled over each other before Avery's failing momentum let them halt on the edge of the drop to the gully. But Avery struggled on top and pinned Rourke's shoulders to the rocky ground.

The two men swayed back and forth as Rourke tried to buck Avery, but when he failed, he chopped both his hands on either side of Avery's neck. The action came with little force, but it was enough to make Avery flinch and using this momentary advantage, Rourke squirmed out from beneath him.

But Avery grabbed a trailing leg, halting his escape.

Rourke kicked out, knocking his hand away, but Avery lunged for his gun instead and swung it round to aim it down at Rourke.

In desperation, Rourke ducked and kicked. A slug

whistled past his shoulder, but his flailing kick crashed into Avery's leg and knocked him to his knees. His gun hand hit rock and ripped the gun from his grip.

Rourke rolled to his knees to face Avery only to receive a solid slug to the jaw that knocked him back and a further flurry of blows that sent him reeling.

'Shoot him!' Rourke yelled from the ground, but no gunfire came.

Rourke rolled over on to his back only to see Avery take a long dive at him. He pushed to the side, seeking to roll away, but still Avery landed heavily on him, blasting all wind from his body.

Gasping, Rourke thrust his legs back, searching for purchase on the hard rock as he tried to thrust himself out from under Avery, but Avery wrapped two large hands around Rourke's neck.

'Shoo—' Rourke murmured, before Avery closed his windpipe.

Rourke slammed his hands on either side of Avery's neck, but this time, the blow had no effect and Avery merely redoubled his efforts. His arms flexed and his jaw muscles bunched as he squeezed.

Desperately, Rourke glanced to the side.

Barton and Dave were struggling with their arms wrapped around each other, rocking back and forth as each man tried to throw the other man to the ground.

With no time to work out what this meant, Rourke threw all his strength into bucking Avery. He kicked out. He thrust up his chest. He stabbed at Avery's eyes.

Avery shrugged away from each action, but only when Rourke wrapped his hands around Avery's neck did Avery's grip slacken a moment, and with this faint hope burgeoning in him, Rourke threw everything into tightening his own grip.

Avery leaned back, trying to rip Rourke's hands away. Rourke hung on, but with Avery's arms stretched to their limit, Rourke released his grip and hurled both his arms outwards, splaying Avery's arms and ripping his hands from his throat.

Free from Avery's grasp, Rourke thrust his legs back and struggled, but Avery still had his whole weight on him and he could do nothing but squirm. Avery rolled his shoulders, then slammed both hands together and crashed them down towards Rourke's head.

But Rourke saw the blow coming and rocked his head away. The blow took a deflective hit off his forehead, then crunched into solid rock.

Avery screeched and fell back, wringing his hands.

Free now, Rourke staggered to his feet and hurled himself at Avery, but Avery turned away from his charge and Rourke fell into a solid shoulder. He rebounded and tumbled on his back.

On the ground, Rourke tried to push up, but his arms failed to hold him and he crashed down on his back again.

Avery smirked and dashed for his gun. On one knee he slipped it into his hand and swung it round to aim it at Rourke.

Rourke glanced around, searching for his own gun, but as it was ten yards away, he could only glare up at Avery as the outlaw stood and sauntered towards him.

With an arrogant smirk plastered across his face, Avery swung to a halt and stared down at him, his feet set wide.

Rourke glanced to his side. Barton had Dave in a firm headlock and was trying to wrestle him to the ground, but then Dave looked up and flinched on seeing Avery standing over Rourke.

'No!' Dave cried.

Barton glanced up too and with a snap of his wrist released Dave.

As Dave collapsed to the ground, Barton stood a moment, then, with a cry and a long tumbling dive, hurled himself at Avery.

Avery twitched, Barton's frantic charge catching him in an indecisive moment and by the time he had firmed his gun hand and blasted at Rourke, Barton slammed into his shoulder, knocking him to the side.

Avery's shot winged past Rourke's head, gouging dirt inches from his forehead, as Barton's momentum bundled Avery into the boulder on the edge of the drop to the gully. With terrible, inevitable slowness, the two men tumbled over the side.

Rourke winced and rushed for his gun, then dashed to the boulder. He peered over it, but he could only watch the two men wheel down the side of the gully before they crashed in a tangled, broken heap at the bottom.

Rourke shook his head and turned to find that Dave had stood and had levelled his gun at his head.

'What you doing?' Rourke asked.

'I don't want to shoot you, but if you force me, I will do it.' Dave firmed his hand. 'Brother, make the right decision and do nothing.'

'I ain't making the decisions here. You're the one with the choices to make.'

'You don't know what my choices are.'

'I don't.' With exaggerated slowness, Rourke batted the dust from his clothes, then folded his arms and glared at Dave. 'But I've spent the last few days trying to second guess you and now that you've pulled a gun on me, I reckon I know the full story. You used me to remove Mendosa's back-up because you've sided with Duttoni to steal Mendosa's rifles.'

'You know nothing. I've sided with Mendosa to get Duttoni's gold.'

'Then I don't understand your plan, but I do know you won't succeed. You're saloon trash, Dave. The likes of Mendosa and Duttoni aren't. When you deal with them, you'll face a new life – and a short one.'

'I know the risks. But this one job will sort everything out.'

'It won't. Taking responsibility will sort your life out. Double-crossing outlaws will just get you killed.' Rourke held his hands wide. 'Do the right thing. I'll forget this conversation happened. Just join me and help me do what you claimed you wanted to do. We'll track down both outlaw gangs. You'll get a share of the reward money, and you'll get it honestly. And the pride you'll gain will change your life.'

Dave shook his head. 'Holster your gun, unhook your belt, and throw it to the side. And don't try anything. I want my nephew to grow up with a pa.'

For long moments Rourke glared at Dave. Then he holstered his gun. With slow movements he unhooked his belt and held it at arm's length.

Rourke swung the belt back and forth, then hurled it at Dave's head. The belt twirled end over end as it whipped through the air, but as Dave ducked from it for it to skid to a halt behind him, Rourke dashed at him.

Dave firmed his gun hand, but as Rourke pounded the last few paces, he still didn't fire. Even so, Rourke piled into him, but at the last moment, Dave ducked and used Rourke's momentum to hurl him over his shoulder.

Rourke hit the ground and rolled. When he came up it was to receive a kick to the jaw that sent him sprawling and another kick to the guts that blasted all the wind from him.

Gasping for air and clutching his guts, he peered up at the advancing Dave.

'Join me,' Rourke whispered, his voice gruff.

Dave lifted his gun hand high.

Rourke glared up as he tried to force his legs to let him rise, but then Dave whirled his arm and he saw the glint of gunmetal slam into his temple, knocking him flat.

Through pain-narrowed eyes, Rourke watched Dave stalk away, but by then darkness was closing fast.

CHAPTER 16

Dave galloped from Snakepass Gully. Whenever he glanced over his shoulder to check that Rourke wasn't following him, the sight of Barton's body flashed back at him and his argument with Rourke seemed to echo down the gully. But he gritted his teeth and headed for Diamond Ridge.

After twenty minutes of hard riding across the plains, he approached the ridge. He veered to the side, aiming for the end of the ridge, but from under a large overhanging rock a rider emerged and galloped towards him. Dave recognized Irwin, but he still rode on for another hundred yards before he pulled his horse to a halt and let Irwin catch up with him.

'You idiot,' Irwin muttered when he pulled alongside. 'If you'd ridden for another half-mile you'd have run straight into Mendosa's gang.'

'Sorry,' Dave murmured, tipping back his hat. 'My mind was elsewhere.'

'What happened? And where's Rourke?'

'We arrested the outlaws. Barton got killed and

Rourke told me to ride on ahead to tell you what had happened while he secures our prisoners.'

Irwin nodded and led him to his hidden vantage point. At the foot of the ridge they dismounted and led their horses on a winding route up the side of the craggy mound of rocks.

When they'd crested the ridge top they tethered their horses; then, with their heads down, they scurried to the other side. They joined Tanner in hunkering down beside a large boulder where they could peer down at the plains beyond.

A wagon was waiting 300 yards out. Four men flanked it.

'Seems Mendosa's still waiting for Duttoni,' Dave said.

'He'll come,' Tanner said.

'Yeah,' Irwin said, glancing over his shoulder at the ridge behind him. 'But I'd feel happier if Rourke were here first.'

'Let's hope he makes it in time for all the fun.' Tanner glanced over Irwin's shoulder and winked at Dave.

Rourke levered himself to his feet and swayed, then firmed his stance and glanced around.

He rubbed his temple, then the back of his head, wincing as his probing fingers brushed what would become several ugly bumps.

Dave had tried to scare away the horses, but Rourke's roving gaze picked out one of the outlaws' horses mooching around at the bottom of the gully.

With no choice, he shuffled and slid down the

gully. At the bottom, he held his hands wide and advanced on the horse, then rushed for the trailing reins.

The horse merely watched him with an appraising eye, then docilely let Rourke lead him when he'd grabbed the reins.

With the reins held securely in his right hand, Rourke looked around.

Arched over a rock was the broken form of Barton. Still, Rourke paced to the body's side and felt the neck. He confirmed that Barton was dead, then stood back a moment with his head bowed.

He turned away and was about to mount the horse, but then reached into his pocket and extracted a spare deputy's badge.

'Good work, Deputy,' he said, pinning the badge on Barton's chest. 'You did a fine job. You're a credit to the badge.'

Then Rourke leapt on the horse and galloped down Snakepass Gully towards Diamond Ridge.

Quinn Mendosa paced from his wagon to face the newly arrived wagon. He stretched his legs after his lengthy sojourn in the wagon while the agreed four men stalked round to flank him.

From the other wagon, Miguel Duttoni emerged and paced towards him until the two men stood ten feet apart.

Four other men swaggered round from the wagon and stood behind Duttoni, their thumbs tucked into their gunbelts and their stances wide.

'Heard plenty about you,' Mendosa said.

With a gloved hand, Duttoni rubbed a finger down a scar on his cheek.

'Ain't heard anything about you,' he grunted. 'So Manuel will look over the merchandise.'

The man at the end strode three paces to stand alongside Duttoni. He looked Mendosa up and down, then spat to the side.

Mendosa snorted. 'And as I've heard plenty about you, Waldo will look over the payment.'

Duttoni flashed a sneer, then nodded. Waldo paced forward to stand by Mendosa.

All four men glared at each other. Then Duttoni snorted.

'So,' he said, folding his arms, 'you reckon you're a gun-runner?'

Mendosa held his hands wide. 'Got the guns. I reckon that's enough.'

'Perhaps, but I run that line of work around these parts.'

'I ain't arguing with you. I just took advantage of an opportunity that came my way.' Mendosa rubbed his jaw. 'Of course, if you like what I have to offer, I can organize another opportunity another day.'

Duttoni sneered, creasing his scar.

'I don't offer long-term deals.'

'And neither do I. But if I come across some guns that need liberating, and you have some gold that you want to give me, we might be able to do business.'

'We might. But that depends on whether I can trust you.'

'If you doubted that, you shouldn't be here.'

'I do doubt it.' Duttoni chuckled, the sound deep and humourless. He narrowed his eyes and inch by inch lowered his hand until it rested on his gunbelt. 'But there's only way to find out what the truth is.'

Behind him, his men edged their hands towards their holsters.

A sly grin invaded Duttoni's scarred face.

CHAPTER 17

At the top of Diamond Ridge, Dave glanced over Irwin's shoulder at Tanner.

Tanner glared back, his forehead and cheeks heavy with sweat.

Dave wiped a layer of sweat from his own brow and returned to staring down at the plains and the two wagons, which were now facing each other.

The plan they'd agreed with Mendosa was for them to wait until Mendosa gave the signal, then start firing, simulating an apparent raid that would force Duttoni to defend himself using whatever back-up he'd hidden elsewhere along Diamond Ridge.

Then, when Mendosa revealed his own back-up, the three of them would sneak off with just the gold.

The money split three ways would satisfy all of them.

But with Duttoni being an hour late, and Dave's failure to find rope to bind Rourke, every second he waited dragged on his nerves.

Then, down below, Mendosa lifted his hat, brushed back his hair, and replaced the hat.

Dave heaved a sigh of relief at seeing the signal, but he still sat silently for another ten seconds. Then he looked up.

'Now,' he murmured.

Irwin glanced at him. 'What?'

As Dave met Irwin's gaze, Tanner swung out from behind his covering rock to stand behind Irwin, his gun stock held high. A dull thud sounded and Irwin keeled over on to his front to reveal Tanner standing behind him. Tanner thrust his gun back into its holster, then dragged Irwin back a few paces from the edge of the ridge.

Dave and Tanner shared nods, then slammed their guns on top of their respective covering boulders. They blasted off a steady burst of gunfire. The gunshots echoed down the ridge. From such a distance all of it was wild but Duttoni flinched and backed, his other men dropping to their haunches to fire indiscriminately in all directions.

Mendosa wheeled back with his men to hide behind his wagon and within moments Duttoni and his men matched their actions. From the safety of their cover neither side took a chance, preferring instead to keep their heads down and fire at unsighted targets.

After their initial burst of gunfire, Dave and Tanner limited themselves to the occasional shot, not daring to risk revealing their location.

'You still having second thoughts?' Tanner asked as he peered down at the wagons.

'Yeah.' Dave rested his forehead on his arm. 'I got Barton killed back in Snakepass Gully.'

Tanner winced. 'Pity, but he decided to risk his life for a share of the reward.'

'Yeah, but all that man wanted was a place to sleep for the night and some honest work. Our scheming got him killed.'

'Ain't nothing we can do about that now. And we'll have the lawmen after us no matter what we do.'

Dave glanced at Tanner. 'But we've done the minimum we agreed to do with Mendosa by starting this gunfight. He doesn't need our help for the rest.'

'You saying we should just turn around and ride away?'

Dave hung his head a moment, then nodded. 'Yeah.'

'We can't,' Tanner said, firming his jaw. 'We started this. We have to end it.'

Dave forced a nod, but then pointed down the side of the ridge.

A line of horses was peeling off from the ridge a half-mile away.

'So that's where Duttoni's back-up were hiding,' he murmured.

With this revelation, Tanner and Irwin kept their heads down until the riders were closing on the wagons. Then they scurried back from the edge of the ridge and dashed for their horses. As the gunfire ripped out anew below, they picked separate routes down the side of the ridge.

Once he was out on the plains, Dave galloped towards the two wagons with Tanner one hundred yards to his side. The new arrivals had positioned themselves around Duttoni's wagon and, with the confidence of their superior numbers, were now taking more risks. In a slight hollow two men were on their bellies and were taking careful aim at Mendosa's wagon with rifles. Two other men were edging out in a long arc to outflank Mendosa's men.

When Dave was around one hundred yards from the wagons, Duttoni yelled to his men and pointed at him. Gunfire ripped through the air around him. With no choice, Dave pulled his horse to a halt and jumped down to hide behind the best cover available on the plains, a hollow.

On his belly, he edged forward until he could see the wagons. Tanner jumped down from his horse and leapt into the hollow a moment later, a burst of gunfire hurrying him on.

For the next two minutes they kept low and watched Mendosa's men and Duttoni's men fire at each other. Then the men who were seeking to outflank Mendosa gained a position square on to the wagon and laid down a ripping burst of gunfire that peppered the side of the wagon.

Mendosa's men hurled themselves beneath the wagon, but gunfire from the rifle-bearers ripped into the wheels.

Mendosa barked orders to each of his men. Then, as his men laid down a huge burst of covering gunfire, he scurried back from the wagon. Gunfire ripped at his heels as he dashed in a long arc towards Dave and Tanner.

Dave and Tanner pulled their guns and fired at Duttoni's men who had strayed from the wagon. Although their shots were high, they forced them to

130

lie low long enough for Mendosa to sprint the last fifty yards and hurl himself into the hollow. On hands and feet he shuffled to lie beside them.

'Lawmen dealt with?' he asked.

'Yup,' Dave said.

Mendosa glanced at Dave. 'Thanks for covering me. You know I couldn't speak up for you, don't you? Waldo would have realized something was wrong if I had.'

'Tanner explained it to me.' Dave provided a reluctant smile. 'Everything else dealt with?'

'Yeah. In another minute, my men will back away in apparent panic and encourage Duttoni's men to take the wagon.'

'And if they don't take the bait?'

Mendosa chuckled. 'I reckon it won't matter how close anyone is.'

Tanner and Dave both nodded and returned to watching the gun battle.

After a minute Mendosa's men slipped out from beneath the wagon and fell back to take a position thirty yards to the rear.

'Fifty seconds,' Mendosa whispered.

Duttoni and half of his men took the opportunity to dash for cover behind Mendosa's wagon.

'Forty seconds.'

Duttoni's men whooped their delight as they trapped their opponents in the open plains.

'Thirty seconds.'

Duttoni's men edged out and fired, then took cover again.

'Twenty seconds.'

Duttoni lifted the flap to Mendosa's wagon and peered inside. He froze. A huge cry ripped from his lips.

Mendosa shuffled down. 'Fifteen seconds.'

Duttoni leapt backwards and landed on his back, but within a moment he was on his feet and hurtling from the wagon, his arms wheeling as he fought for more speed.

'Ten seconds.'

Duttoni's men glanced at each other, shrugging, then dashed after him.

'Five seconds.'

Two of Mendosa's men followed Duttoni's mad dash, ripping gunfire at his back, but the other two men, Waldo and Eli, stared at them, agog.

Mendosa chuckled to himself.

'Duck,' he whispered.

As one, Mendosa, Dave and Tanner pressed their noses into the dirt and slammed their hands over their ears. Even so, the huge series of explosions echoed in Rourke's ears and a grit-filled gale blew his hat off.

He rescued his hat and peered up. The dust and debris was still rising. Mendosa's rifle-laden, and unbeknown to anyone but them, dynamite-laden, wagon had obliterated itself. And from the burning and wrecked state of Duttoni's wagon, Dave didn't expect either group of outlaws to have survived.

'Let's just hope that gold doesn't burn,' he said.

'It don't.' Mendosa stood, laughing and flexing his knees. 'And that explosion was almost worth the two weeks I spent guarding my wagon.'

They paced towards the wrecked wagons. Splinters and burnt cloth cascaded around them, but the wind whipped the smoke to the side, letting them view the carnage ahead. And they saw nothing but bodies.

They paced to within thirty yards of Duttoni's wagon, but a gunshot blasted over their heads. They hunkered down, peering left and right as they searched for the location of the shooter, but then Waldo and Eli leapt up from behind a rock twenty yards from Mendosa's wrecked wagon.

Eli's right sleeve was still smouldering and soot blackened both men's faces, but this didn't slow them as they hurtled towards them, firing at every pace.

'Double-crossers,' Waldo roared and fired again.

Dave leapt to the ground and ripped his gun from its holster.

Waldo dashed towards him and, with no choice, Dave fired. With his poor gunfighting ability, the shot was wild. At his side, Tanner stood hunched and blasted at Waldo too, but Waldo slid to a halt and ripped out an arc of gunfire that cut a swathe through Tanner's guts and spun him round and to the ground.

Waldo twitched a finger on an empty chamber, snorted, then hurtled at Dave.

Dave glanced to the side to see that Mendosa and Eli were ripping gunfire at each other from ten yards apart. Then he rolled on to one knee and got in one last wild shot before Waldo hurled himself at him. He bundled into him, knocking him to the ground.

With his eyes blazing, Waldo kicked Dave's gun

away, then hurled himself on top of him and wrapped both hands around Dave's neck.

Dave threw his hands to Waldo's hands and tried to prise them away, but Waldo threw his weight behind his grip, his eyes wild and spit dribbling from his mouth.

Flickers of intermittent light and darkness played around Dave.

In desperation Dave gripped Waldo's fingers and pulled them back, but Waldo just pulled Dave to his feet and braced himself as he tightened his grip on Dave's throat. For long moments Waldo hung on, but then he rolled his shoulders to get a firmer grip. Using this chance, Dave settled his stance, then kicked Waldo's legs from under him.

Waldo hit the ground and rolled, then leapt to his feet but it was only to walk into a desperate lunging blow from Dave. Waldo tumbled on to his back and skidded, only coming to a halt when he slammed into Tanner's prone body.

Waldo snickered at his good fortune and fumbled over Tanner's body to prise his gun from his dead fingers. He ripped the gun to the side to aim it at Dave, but Dave threw himself flat and the shot skidded by his head.

Dave righted himself and leapt for his gun. His scrambling fingers closed on the metal and in desperation he rolled on to his back and fired at Waldo, aiming low. His wild shot ripped past his trailing left foot, but scythed into Waldo's leg, spinning him to his knees.

Dave rolled to his haunches and took more careful

aim. Just as Waldo sighted him down the barrel of his gun he fired, blasting lead into Waldo's guts. The slug knocked Waldo back and around, a last finger-twitch ripping a useless gunshot into the air before he keeled over on to his back.

Waldo twitched once, then was still.

Dave glanced around. Gunfire was ripping out from Duttoni's wagon, and Mendosa and Eli had closed on each other and were slugging it out.

Dave trained his gun on Eli, but Mendosa was winning this fight.

Mendosa held Eli upright while he hammered a fist into his guts, then stood back while Eli folded. He rolled his shoulders, then slammed an uppercut to his jaw that lifted his feet from the ground before he crashed down on his back.

As Eli lay, stunned and supine, Mendosa whirled round to Dave.

'Shoot him,' he shouted.

Dave trained his gun on Eli, but couldn't force his trigger finger to move, and with a snort, Mendosa ripped out his gun, reloaded, and blasted three slugs into Eli.

Mendosa glanced at the wagons. His eyes narrowed as like Dave he searched for who was firing, then shrugged and hunkered down beside Dave.

'What you reckon?' he asked.

Dave pointed beyond Duttoni's wagon, the devastated remnants still indistinct in the smoke.

'I reckon Duttoni and four of his men are over there. So we still got a fight to get that gold.'

Mendosa snorted and edged forward.

'Yeah, but—'

A huge rumble of gunfire blasted nearby, but this time coming from the direction of Diamond Ridge. Dave glanced over his shoulder.

'I reckon I spoke too soon,' he murmured.

Mendosa turned to see where Dave was looking.

A line of ten riders was hurtling towards the wagons from the ridge, guns thrust out, the firing constant and closing.

'I should have guessed,' Mendosa muttered. 'Duttoni has a second back-up.'

Dave narrowed his eyes, then gulped.

'No, that ain't Duttoni's back-up,' he murmured. 'It's worse. It's Marshal Devine.'

With his grogginess receding with each mile, Rourke made good time, but as he approached Diamond Ridge, gunfire from ahead confirmed his worst fears. He gritted his teeth and galloped on ahead.

Then a huge explosion ripped through the air, echoing and rippling around the ridge.

When the echoes had faded to stillness, sporadic gunfire blasted and Rourke spurred his horse for even greater speed.

As he neared the edge of the ridge, smoke flurried from behind the craggy rocks and when he emerged on to the plains, two devastated wagons were on fire. Bodies lay sprawled and bloody over rocks and flat on the ground. A huddle of four men knelt on the ground with their hands on their heads. Set before them was a line of riders. These men turned to face Rourke. One man peeled away and approached.

Rourke pulled his gun and slowed his pace, looking for cover, but then saw the barred cell that stood beside the wagons. Then even more assurance came when he recognized the man riding towards him through the swirling smoke as the huge form of Marshal Jake T. Devine.

Rourke holstered his gun and raised a hand to the approaching rider.

'Howdy, Devine,' he shouted.

Devine pulled his horse to a halt and waited for him to draw alongside.

'Howdy,' he grunted. 'You got here too late. All the fun's over.'

'Everyone rounded up?'

'Got Mendosa. Killed Duttoni.' Devine grinned and spat to the side. 'The others are either rounded up or dead.'

Rourke nodded. With Devine at his side he approached the tangle of defeated prisoners sitting before the burnt-out wagons. As all the men had their heads bowed, and many were blackened with soot, he didn't recognize any of them, so he peered at each body that he passed.

He saw Tanner lying sprawled on his back with gunshots ripped across his guts. He shifted his gaze to the next body, knowing in a guilty way that he was more concerned to see whether Irwin was amongst the fallen than Dave.

His gaze passed over the last three bodies, then centred on the captured men.

One of the men looked up and for just a moment, he and Dave shared eye contact, then Rourke turned away to face Devine.

He was about to ask whether he'd seen Irwin when he saw another rider approach from Diamond Ridge. Rourke narrowed his eyes, then sighed when he recognized his deputy.

With a smile on his lips, Rourke told Devine who the arrival was, then peeled away to talk to him.

Fifty yards from the wagons, Irwin pulled his horse to a halt. He glanced at the burnt-out wagons and the prisoners, then turned to Rourke.

'Dave knocked me out,' he said, fingering the back of his head.

Rourke snorted and prodded at the back of his own head.

'Seems he has a habit of doing that.'

The two lawmen nodded to each other, then joined Devine in appraising the captured men. Rourke pointedly avoided catching Dave's eye.

'You need help?' he asked.

'Nope,' Devine said. 'I can chain up these varmints before heading to Stone Creek.'

'But I thought you'd be heading back to Beaver Ridge.'

'Ain't no point in serving justice if nobody sees that justice.' Devine pointed to the mobile cell. 'Before I take them in, everyone in Stone Creek can see them in chains. The dead ones can rot where they fell.'

Rourke sneered, but knowing that he wasn't hiding his disgust, tipped his hat to Devine, then trotted away with Irwin at his side.

'Get back to Stone Creek,' he said when they were

out of Devine's earshot, 'and get Andy to collect these bodies.'

Irwin nodded. 'You staying to tell Devine that Dave's your brother?'

'Nope. I'm heading to Snakepass Gully. Got a deputy to pick up.' Rourke turned his horse. 'And that man was worth ten of Dave.'

CHAPTER 18

With Barton's and the outlaws' bodies draped over the backs of their horses and trailing behind him, Rourke returned to Diamond Ridge.

Andy Scrothers, Stone Creek's undertaker, and five helpers from Stone Creek were loading the last dead outlaw on to a cart.

Devine and his prisoners were long gone.

Rourke joined them and the sombre cortège trundled across the plains towards Stone Creek.

Everybody maintained a respectful silence until they rode into town.

For maximum effect Devine had pulled up his mobile cell outside the Golden Star.

Inside the cell the remaining defeated outlaws huddled, their short chains constraining their movements to less than a foot in any direction. None of the arrogance that Mendosa was famed for was apparent as he sat hunched, staring at his manacled wrists.

A crowd had gathered on the boardwalk and stood with drinks in hand, engaged in animated conversation as they eyed the captured outlaws.

'Animals,' Irwin muttered.

'You mean the outlaws,' Rourke said, 'Devine for doing this, or the townsfolk for watching?'

'All of them.' Irwin snorted and headed to the sheriff's office.

Rourke rode past the mobile cell, pointedly averting his gaze, and stopped outside Foster Cartwright's store. He wandered in to the store to find Foster and Celeste standing behind the counter, shaking their heads and muttering under their breaths.

'Can't you stop Devine's show?' Celeste asked while they shared a quick hug.

'I can't,' Rourke said, stepping back. 'If Devine wants to parade his victory, I can't stop him. Is Harlan with you?'

'Yes. He's in the back, but he knows they're out there – and who is out there.'

'Upset?'

'As you'd expect.'

Rourke sighed. 'Should we let Harlan see Dave before he leaves?'

'I'm surprised you asked.'

'Been thinking about the things you said. Dave's advice to Harlan wasn't all that bad. It was pretty much what an uncle should say to a nephew when asked.' Rourke sighed. 'But that's the problem.'

Celeste nodded. 'You don't want Harlan wondering why a man who was kind to him gets chained up and dragged off to Beaver Ridge to hang?'

'Yeah. I can't answer that. I know Dave can't, but . . .' Rourke held his hands wide. 'What you reckon?'

'Understanding Dave's fate might be a good lesson for him.' She nodded to Rourke and Rourke moved to walk past her, but she raised a hand, halting him. 'But afterwards, we shouldn't let him have any more good lessons for a while.'

Rourke nodded and headed into the back store.

Harlan was sitting hunched on a barrel, scuffing his feet on the floor.

'You all right?' Rourke asked.

'Not really,' Harlan whimpered and rubbed his snuffling nose on his sleeve.

'You know what's happening outside?'

'I do, but why did Uncle . . .' Harlan rubbed his red-rimmed eyes. 'Why did he do it?'

'I don't know.' Rourke knelt beside Harlan and laid a comforting hand on his back. 'But maybe you can ask him.'

Harlan lowered his head. A single tear splashed on the floor at his feet.

'I don't want to.'

'You might not want to. But you should still do it.'

With a wandering foot, Harlan scuffed the tear away, then looked up.

'Then I will. It's the grown-up thing to do.'

To Rourke's nod, Harlan shuffled off the barrel and together they left the storeroom.

When they reached the door Rourke glanced at Celeste, but she returned a nod and so they paced outside and down the boardwalk.

Rourke rested a hand on Harlan's shoulder until they stood before the mobile cell, but as Devine wasn't there, Rourke hailed Deputy Carter.

'Where's Devine?' he asked.

'Holding court in the saloon,' Carter said.

Rourke nodded and glanced over his shoulder into the Golden Star.

A crowd bustled around the doors, guffaws and bellowing emerging from within.

Rourke glanced at the cell, then shrugged.

'And where's D...? Not all the prisoners are here.'

'We put one of them in your cells – until we move on out.'

Rourke was about to ask why, but then shrugged and shepherded Harlan down the road and into his office.

Inside, Dave was in the central cell. Irwin was sitting on his desk with his arms folded watching him.

Rourke placed both hands on Harlan's shoulders and knelt beside him.

'When you talk to Dave,' he said, 'stay ten feet back from the bars at all times. Understand?'

Harlan nodded and with an encouraging pat on the back from Rourke, he paced by him towards the cell while Rourke backed to stand beside Irwin's desk.

'Howdy, nephew,' Dave said, leaning back against the wall.

'Why did you do it?' Harlan asked, snuffling back a tear.

'That's a long story and I ain't sure I got enough time to tell you it. But I suppose I just got greedy and took what I thought was the easy option.' Dave glanced up at Rourke, then lowered his gaze to Harlan and smiled. 'But as you can see, when you don't do what your pa tells you to do, you end up in a cell.'

'I don't know why Pa's locked you up, but I didn't mean that.' Harlan took a deep breath, then slammed his hands on his hips and raised his voice. 'I mean you stole my dollar.'

'I stole your . . . Ah, that.'

'You told me that if I invested my dollar in a secret place it'd grow into two dollars, but when I looked this afternoon, it'd gone. And I reckon you stole it.'

Dave sighed and rolled to his feet. 'I can't lie to you. I did that.'

'Why?' Harlan whispered.

In his outstretched hands, Dave grabbed two bars and pressed his face in the gap between them. He sneered.

'I did it because you're an idiot,' he muttered, his voice harsh. 'You may think you're all grown up, but you're just a whining little brat who's looking for someone with more sense to come along and use you. The sooner you grow up and stop snivelling, the better it'll be for all—'

'That's enough,' Rourke shouted, pacing to Harlan's side.

Harlan opened and closed his mouth. Then, with a sob, he dashed past Rourke to the door. Rourke moved to grab him, but Irwin shook his head.

'I'll take him back to the store,' he said. 'After that, I reckon you'll have something to say to Dave.'

Rourke nodded. He watched Irwin rest a hand on

Harlan's back and direct him outside, then turned.

Dave pushed back from the bars and folded his arms as Rourke paced across the room to stand before him.

'That make you feel better?' Rourke muttered. 'You just bullied a boy half your size and twice your decency.'

'I just said what you wanted me to say.' Dave flared his eyes and lowered his voice to a gruff mutter. 'If you listen to evil Dave's advice, you'll end up in a cell like this one.'

'You're right. I did bring him here so that he could hear that. But I didn't bring him here so that you could shout at him.'

'Harsh lessons need harsh words.' Dave slumped on his bunk. 'You don't have to thank me now, but what I said will do him some good.'

'Don't try to sound honourable. It doesn't work with you.' Rourke snorted. 'I don't know what Harlan meant, but it sounds like you stole off him, then blamed him.'

'I wasn't blaming him. Harlan's old enough to ask about girls, but he's so naïve, he thinks that if you bury a dollar, it'll grow into two dollars.' Dave sneered. 'Now he'll avoid anyone else scamming him.'

'He's only a kid. He'll learn those lessons when he needs to.'

'He might, but sometimes kids have their naïvety blasted out of them a lot more rudely than just having a dollar stolen off them.'

'Another typical excuse from you. You had some

tough breaks so that explains why you're facing the noose back in Beaver Ridge.'

Dave clattered his feet on his bunk and lay back, staring at the ceiling.

Rourke glared down at him, waiting for him to look his way so he could continue the argument, but Dave began whistling under his breath.

Behind him, the door opened and Irwin paced into the office, so with a last glare down at Dave, Rourke left his office and hurried down the road.

In Cartwright's store, Celeste was comforting a weeping Harlan.

'I'm sorry,' Rourke said as he halted. 'I thought it'd do some good.'

'It still might,' she said as she cleaned Harlan's face with the corner of a kerchief. 'But don't worry about that now. I'll get home early. Hanging round in town with that cell outside isn't healthy for anyone.'

Rourke nodded and walked them outside and to their cart, keeping his body between them and the mobile cell. He tossled Harlan's hair, then lifted him on the cart.

With a last thin smile to Celeste, he stood on the boardwalk and watched them trundle down the road.

When they disappeared beyond the last building, Rourke turned and strode to the Golden Star, determined to order Devine to leave his town. But as he arrived, Devine swaggered from the saloon and with a few barked commands to Deputy Carter, cleared the space ahead and organized the mobile cell to leave town.

Rourke stood back and watched the deputies take positions at the four corners of the cell.

As Devine took the lead, Carter strode into the sheriff's office and returned with Dave in tow, but instead of locking him in the cell with the other prisoners, he tied his hands behind his back and levered him on to the back of a horse.

Carter tipped his hat to Rourke and turned to leave town, but Rourke wandered up to Devine.

'Why are you keeping that man separate?'

'Ain't no business of yours,' Devine grunted. 'But seeing as you asked so nicely, the other prisoners have got it into their heads that he double-crossed them, especially Mendosa, so I'm keeping him separate until he gets to swing in Beaver Ridge.'

Devine gestured to his deputies and at an orderly trot the cortège headed off.

Just as the cell lurched to a start, Dave glanced over his shoulder at Rourke and provided a wan smile.

Rourke returned a firm-jawed stare.

For long moments he stood in the road watching the mobile cell leave town, then turned and headed to the sheriff's office.

CHAPTER 19

For fifteen minutes Rourke discussed what Devine had just told him with Irwin.

Irwin saw nothing odd about Devine keeping Dave separate, figuring that Rourke was incapable of being objective where Dave was concerned. Rourke accepted this, but after another fifteen minutes of brooding on his own in his office, he wandered outside and mounted his horse.

At a steady trot he rode back to his house. Conflicting thoughts rattled through his mind, but when he arrived home ten minutes after Celeste and Harlan, he still had no solution to his problem.

Inside, he looked in on Harlan, but his son lay on his bed, staring at the ceiling, and was unresponsive to all his questions.

Rourke relented and returned to the main room.

'Just give him a while to think things through,' Celeste said.

Rourke nodded, then drew Ccleste to sit facing him at the table. He told her about the raid, ending with Devine's decision to hold Dave separately and

Mendosa's hatred of Dave.

'That could mean plenty of things,' she said.

'It could. But I ain't sure what happened between Mendosa blowing up the wagons and Devine arriving to arrest everyone. Did Mendosa just blame Dave for their plans failing? Or did Dave finally realize how much wrong he'd done and turn on Mendosa and help to get him arrested?'

'If he helped, he wouldn't keep quiet about it.'

'Dave's devious. If he claimed he helped, I wouldn't believe him. So the only way he could convince me that he helped was to say nothing.'

'That reasoning is far too convoluted. But if you reckon there's a chance you're right, you have to speak to Marshal Devine.'

'I can't. Not after keeping quiet when he left. And after all the risks I took in agreeing to Dave's and Tanner's plan, speaking up now would risk my career. And Dave ain't worth that.'

'I don't agree. You have to do something.'

For another hour Celeste and he discussed his problem. But still with no clear solution other than the fact that he had to do something, he wandered into the bedroom and changed his clothes, then left his house and mounted his horse. Celeste followed him outside.

'What you planning to do?' she asked.

'Don't know,' Rourke said, tipping back his hat. 'But I kind of hope that by the time I catch up with Devine, I might have figured it out.'

Rourke grabbed the reins and galloped from his home.

A mile out of town, Rourke picked up Devine's trail and followed it at a gallop.

His mind stayed in a fugue right up until the moment he saw the cortège trundling down the trail before him.

The pitiful sight of the outlaws, chained like animals and hunched in the cell, convinced him that if there was a chance that the man riding behind the mobile cell was innocent, he had to do something – even if that rider was his worthless brother and even if he was risking his career and his life.

He headed off the trail, circled round, and waited three miles further on in Skull Pass. As trying to persuade a man like Devine to release Dave was a hopeless venture, he had to use the only language Devine would understand. So Rourke removed a kerchief from his pocket and wrapped it over his mouth.

When the cortége was level with him, he strode out from his covering rock.

'Devine,' he shouted, deliberately grating his voice. 'Stop there. You're surrounded.'

Devine twitched and glanced around, his hand whirling towards his holster, but Rourke fired a warning shot over his head. Devine raised his hand, but his firm gaze fell on Rourke.

'You've made a big mistake,' Devine roared. 'Nobody threatens me and lives.'

'We ain't threatening you. We just want one of your prisoners – the man on horseback.'

Devine held his hands wide. 'Then come down and get him.'

'Just leave him here and ride on ahead.'

Devine spat to the side. 'He's swinging in Beaver Ridge.'

'We don't want him to live that long.' Rourke forced a laugh. 'What we plan for him will make him pray to swing.'

Devine chuckled and glanced back at the other prisoners.

'Don't let that varmint go,' Mendosa roared from the cell, rattling his chains. 'I want to see him die.'

Devine turned to look at Rourke. 'That man's right popular.'

'And from the sound of it, he'll be more trouble than you need on a long journey to Beaver Ridge. Leave him here and let us deal with him.'

Devine beckoned Deputy Carter to draw alongside and they exchanged low words.

Carter shook his head repeatedly but Devine snorted and ordered Carter to release Dave's horse. Without further word, Devine then gestured for the cortège to ride on ahead, leaving Dave alone and glancing in all directions. Devine didn't look Rourke's way again.

Rourke tipped back his hat in surprise. He'd expected Devine to resist and was all set for the hardest fight of his life, but he'd heard so many stories about that lawman, and none of them was good.

Still, he waited until the cortège had passed beyond the edge of Skull Pass, a good mile away, then rode down on to the plains.

Dave watched his slow descent, nodding to himself, then rolled from his horse and turned to present him with his bound hands.

Rourke said nothing as he released Dave's bonds, then stood back and mounted his horse. He pointed north and both men galloped towards Snakepass Gully.

After thirty minutes of hard riding, and no talking, they reached the gully.

When they were 400 yards into the gully Rourke told Dave to backtrack along their route until they emerged on to the edge of the plains. Then he directed him to head for a crag and a tangle of boulders fifty feet above ground level – this position was difficult to see from any direction and so was one of his favourite secure points.

As Dave tethered their horses, Rourke dashed into the gully and slapped away their prints leading towards this hiding-place, then hurried back to their cover.

Quietly, they waited and sure enough, twenty minutes later, Devine rode towards them, following their trail. They ducked and let him pass. When his horse had clopped by, they looked up and watched him head further down the gully.

'I knew that was too easy,' Rourke said.

'He'll figure out where we went before too long,' Dave mused. 'And I've heard it said that Devine never loses a man.'

Rourke nodded. 'And I've heard it said that no man who crosses him lives.'

With his gaze still on the plains, Dave rubbed his chin.

'So, brother, why did you take on Devine to rescue me?'

Rourke tipped back his hat to rub his sparse hair, then shrugged.

'I got my reasons.' Rourke turned to face Dave and fixed him with a firm gaze. 'And as I have, you owe me the truth for once in your life.'

'Then I'll tell you.' Dave stared down into the gully. 'I didn't break that window in the Gold—'

Rourke snorted, grabbed Dave's shoulder, and spun him round to face him.

'I didn't mean that. I mean about what you did when Devine arrested Mendosa.'

'The truth about that,' Dave murmured, 'ain't that easy to explain, especially when I don't know what it was myself.'

'But you did turn on Mendosa?'

'I did.'

'Then I was right to save you if you helped Devine with his arrest.'

Dave rubbed his bristled chin and glanced away from Rourke.

'I'd like to say I helped Devine, but the truth is, when that lead started blasting from the marshal, I panicked. When I turned on Mendosa I was just saving my own hide. If I helped to arrest him, it wasn't my intent.' Dave looked at Rourke, his eyes watery. 'Sorry, brother.'

'Don't be. For the first time I've heard an honest answer from you, and as such I reckon I was right to save you. If you've seen what real trouble looks like, you might avoid it in the future.'

'I might at that.' Dave smiled. 'So what do you want me to do now?'

'I don't care. I just expect you to put as much distance as you can between yourself and Devine.'

'That man is relentless. You have to help me get away.'

'I won't. I've given you this one chance. The rest is up to you.' Rourke glared at Dave. 'But if you escape and you don't take it, I'll find you and ensure you do swing.'

'I thought as much, brother.'

Rourke let the smallest of smiles crease his mouth.

'Don't get me wrong, but I hope I never see you again.' Rourke tipped his hat and turned. He stood a moment, then turned back. 'Brother.'

Rourke mounted his horse. He swung it out from the covering rocks and glanced down the gully, then into the plains.

He saw no one, so at a gallop, he headed back to Stone Creek.

He didn't look back.

CHAPTER 20

Dave watched Rourke's form until it disappeared into the shimmering horizon.

Stone Creek was to the south and Devine had headed north, so he looked east and west. Either direction would probably contain trouble now that he was a wanted man, but as he'd probably spend the rest of his life running, he decided he had enough time to think carefully about his next move.

As he pondered, Dave hunkered down behind a covering rock and slipped a hand in his pocket, but as Devine had claimed his knife, he couldn't whittle wood, so he leaned back and looked to the sky.

Slowly, a smile invaded his face.

'Perhaps you were right, brother,' he said.

He shuffled out from the secure position and edged down to the gully bottom, then hid behind a large rock.

For long minutes he sat back against the rock,

unsure whether his sudden decision was the right one, but when he heard hoofs clopping down Snakepass Gully, he lifted to see Devine heading back towards him, then ducked and nodded to himself.

When the hoofs clopped by his rock, he swung his gun on the top of the rock and stood.

'Get those hands up,' he shouted.

Devine pulled his horse to a halt and lifted his hands, but only to chest high.

'Once you'd escaped you should have got some distance instead of waiting to take me on.' Devine chuckled. 'Not that it'd have done you any good.'

'I ain't here to take you on. I just want to talk.'

'Talk away.'

'Not yet. I want you to dismount, sit cross-legged, and get those hands real high. Then we can have that talk.'

From under a louring brow Devine glared back, but then nodded and with deliberate slowness, swung down from his horse. He stalked five paces, then flopped to the ground and slammed his hands on his head.

Dave edged out from behind his rock and levelled his gun at Devine's head.

Devine glared down the barrel of the gun. He chuckled.

'You just made your last mistake, scum. Now you won't live long enough to swing in Beaver Ridge.'

'I'm not threatening you. I'm just keeping this gun on you until you've heard me talk.'

Devine's eyes narrowed to streaks of ice.

'Dead men don't talk.'

'I'm not dead.'

'Ain't you?'

'Devine, I just want to tell you something.'

Devine spat to the side. 'Then do it.'

Dave strode ten paces to stand five yards before Devine. He took a deep breath.

'I want to tell you about my life – about how I got involved in something that was bigger than I expected, about how a boy showed some respect until I disappointed him, about how I wanted to do the right thing, but was so confused about what the right thing was, I didn't know how to do it.'

'And when you've bored me with that story?'

'I'll throw my gun on the ground, back ten paces, sit cross-legged, and place my hands on my head. Then it's up to you what you do next.'

'You're either mighty stupid or mighty sure I'll like your story.'

'Either way, my brother kept on telling me that I had to take responsibility for my actions, and now seems a good time to start.' Dave shrugged. 'And once you've heard everything, I reckon I'll still go to jail, but I don't reckon the law will kill me for telling the truth.'

'You reckon?' Devine lowered his hands to hold them wide. He appraised Dave's shaking gun hand, then licked his lips. 'Sooner you talk, sooner we can end this.'

Dave strode forward another pace.

'I guess it started last week when Barton May threw a chair through the Golden Star's window.' Dave sighed and hung his head a moment. 'No. It started when I threw a chair through the Golden Star's window.'